THE PIANO MAKER

ALSO BY KURT PALKA

Rosegarden
The Chaperon
Equinox
Scorpio Moon
Clara (originally published as *Patient Number 7*)
The Hour of the Fox

KURT PALKA

The
PIANO
MAKER

A Novel

McCLELLAND & STEWART

LIBRARY AND ARCHIVES CANADA CATALOGUING IN PUBLICATION DATA
is available upon request

ISBN: 978-0-7710-7128-7
ebook ISBN: 978-0-7710-7141-6

Typeset in Van Dijck by M&S, Toronto
Printed and bound in USA

McClelland & Stewart,
a division of Random House of Canada Limited,
a Penguin Random House Company
www.penguinrandomhouse.ca

8   9   10   22

Penguin
Random House
McCLELLAND & STEWART

For Heather

And for Melanie and Christina and Aviana and Annie

The Arrival

One

ON THE LAST STRETCH through the coastal forest, the trees stood so close together that hardly any light showed between them. In places they overarched the road like a tunnel, tall evergreens and a few hardwoods, bare this time of year. Nearer to the French Shore the trees then thinned, and eventually they opened up to a fantastic vista to her right, with ocean spray like a billowing fog full of rainbows.

The first village she came to was called Bonne Marie. Halfway through it a dog saw the car, and it barked and came running alongside. She slowed and swerved to avoid it, and not far away a man looked up from the boat hull he was scraping. He called to the dog and immediately it obeyed and stopped. In the mirror she saw it standing in the road, lifting its nose.

For a moment she thought the dog might be Jack, and she stepped on the brake and stared into the mirror, but then she drove on. How could it be Jack? Of course it was not. Even if it had half an ear missing and looked like a northern breed.

She drove past weathered boulders and enormous stone slabs like the remains of an ancient dolmen right by the roadside. Then came more villages: Sainte Emilie, Gaillard, La Roche. Past houses with painted shutters; past some kind of mill or press driven by a donkey. She saw a smithy where a massive brown horse stood with one hind leg on a rest while the farrier worked his file around the hoof. She saw fishing boats on cradles and nets hanging on racks. Here and there someone raised an arm and waved as she drove by.

She saw a few churches, but only small wooden ones, and she kept looking out for the stone tower of Saint Homais. Madame Cabayé in Montreal had suggested the French Shore and especially the town of Saint Homais. She said she'd grown up there and loved it: the people, the fine church, the views. It was still mostly French, she said, but not exclusively any more. A town just big enough and friendly enough for someone to try and make a new home.

"They might never have seen it in the newspaper," Madame Cabayé had said. She'd not looked at her while saying it. And a moment later, still not looking at her, she'd added, "Or if they did, it'll be long forgotten. I can give you a few names."

Ocean spray misted the windshield, and the road was slippery in places. But she felt safe in the car. It was comfortable and well made, her one remaining luxury in these lean times: an Austin Burnham Saloon with a rosewood dash and red leather seats. It had good American whitewall tires and chrome spoke wheels. Four years ago she'd paid cash for it because she'd felt flush then and confident that the money would keep coming. All those buying trips with Nathan. The horse and rider in the Persian bog alone could have paid for seven or eight cars like this.

A November day, cold and clean; the sun's arc shallow, the bright dazzle on the Bay of Fundy broken only by the long, thin ridge of the Digby Neck. It was almost eleven o'clock when she caught the first glint of the tall steeple in the distance, the sun on the silvered slate roof.

She parked on the carriage lot and then walked the town, the cobbled streets and dirt lanes with frozen horseshoe prints and cart tracks in them. She stopped frequently to admire the old houses of dressed stone and wood, some of the timbered gables with dates carved into them two hundred years ago. She saw the hotel that Madame Cabayé had mentioned, a wide building on the main square. A sky-blue sundial with black Roman numerals on the front over the painted name: HÔTEL YAMOUSSOUKE.

When she came to the church, she paused at the doorway in the west front and looked at the details in the arch, the gargoyles in the gutter corners. She stepped inside. From the row of windows along one wall, sunlight fell in coloured shafts on wooden pews, and between the windows hung paintings of the stations of the cross. The pictures were dark, nearly as dark as the frames that contained them.

Straight ahead, placed slightly off-centre on the crossing, there stood a piano, and even from that distance she could tell that it was a Molnar grand. She walked up to it, and as she did so she began to wonder at this strange grouping of events: first Madame Cabayé pointing her to Saint Homais, then the dog that looked like Jack, and now a Molnar waiting for her in this stone place.

The piano's fallboard was up, and so was the lid. She stepped close and looked for the master stamp on the transom. There it was: green ink, faded but still readable. The letters B.R. in a small oval ring.

Morris the sexton saw her from the shadows by the side altar, and within the hour he was telling people that there was something unusual about her. He had watched her walking towards the piano, he said, not a young woman any more but still nice-looking in her city coat and hat. She studied the piano, and then she undid a few buttons on her coat and sat down on the bench with her fingers poised above the keys but not touching them, and for a long moment she looked as though a spell had come over her. She looked stricken and years older suddenly, and it was when she stood up and closed the keyboard and walked away that he saw she had a limp.

He said it had not been noticeable before, but now there

was no doubt about it. There was a darkness to her suddenly. Like a great sadness.

She learned all this later from Mildred Yamoussouke, because Mildred had been in the kitchen at the hotel when Morris told the story to a maid. He'd come to pick up the priest's lunch, and Mildred reached out quickly and closed the door.

"You keep your voice down, Morris," she said. "She's in our dinin' room right now."

"She's from Quebec," he whispered. "It's on the licence plate."

"Hush now," said Mildred. "Be quiet and get on your way before Father's food gets cold."

In the afternoon Morris saw her again in the church. She stood looking at the notice board, and when he came up and asked if he could help with something, she pointed at the slip of paper where Father William was asking for an experienced piano player to help with the church music while the organ was out of service.

"Is he the priest?" she said.

"Yes, he is."

"Do you think I could speak with him?"

"I don't see why not. He's in the vestry now. I can show you the way."

Morris liked her smile when she nodded and said thank you. He led the way down the nave, across the sanctuary and around the altar to the back rooms, and when she was in there with the door closed he listened to them talking for a while, the Father asking questions and she answering.

Eventually Morris returned to his chores, and not long thereafter he saw Father William showing her to the piano. She was carrying her coat and hat, and she put them down in a front pew. She wore her hair up. It was mostly black but there was some grey in it. She gave the piano bench a few turns of the crank to adjust the height and then she sat down. The Father took a pew further back.

Morris was on a stepladder by the north windows. He'd been repairing some of the leading, and when she began to play he turned off the soldering lamp and set it on the ledge and listened.

He thought she was playing very well, and then from the way the Father sat back and relaxed Morris could tell that she had just passed the test.

Afterward she walked back to the hotel and asked to see a room that was quiet. The landlady handed her the number 308 key and smiled at her. "Top floor, out back. Just evergreens and the ocean. My name is Mildred. If there's anything you need, just ask."

"Thank you. Madame Cabayé in Montreal mentioned you to me. And this hotel."

"Our Sidonie? You know her!"

"Yes, I do. I stayed at the *pension* a few times."

"They got married here, but then they moved away."

"She told me. Her husband works at the bank, the Sherbrooke branch. He's the assistant manager and she looks after the *pension*." She raised the key. "We can talk later."

Up in the room she patted the bed and looked around at the armoire and the nightstand painted in a grey-blue with clouds and sunflowers in the French country style; the bathroom through the open door; the view out the window. The silence.

"It's wonderful," she said to Mildred back downstairs. "Thank you. I'll take it. My name is Hélène Giroux. If someone could help me get my luggage from the car? There's a trunk in the backseat that I'll need a hand with."

"Oh, surely," said Mildred. "Let's go and get it."

At seven o'clock that evening she was at the piano again, for the funeral mass for three fishermen.

Mildred had said that every last person in town had known the men and that the church would be full. It was. If she turned to her right she could see the crowded pews and aisles, and everywhere people were staring at her and then whispering to each other and looking at her again, clearly wondering who she was. Mildred had predicted that as well. Now Mildred was sitting in the third pew in the middle, next to her four hotel employees.

Up in the pulpit Father William spoke about the dead men and the loss to their families and to the community.

She sat on the piano bench, waiting, rubbing her hands and keeping them warm in her lap.

Then Father William came down the winding stairs and he looked her way and nodded, and she straightened up and began to play.

Two

THAT NIGHT SHE HAD one of the dreams. She heard Nathan calling her name, but she could not see him. The place he was calling from was all darkness and blood in the snow, and when she called back her breath froze in the air and her words fell to the ground and broke into pieces. It was one of the three or four dreams since the accident that kept repeating: that cave of horror, shadowy movements and smells and pleas that still wrung her heart with each renewed dreaming even though she knew the outcome well by now, and no matter how much she tried in her dreams to change it, she could not. It came on without mercy like blows to a terrified child, and only rarely did she wake before it happened. But that night she did. She woke with a cry and lay staring at the ceiling with her heart hammering, and she sat up and looked around at yet another room in yet another town.

A pale silver light, furniture she did not know.

She threw off the covers and climbed out of bed and stumbled to the window, barefoot on the wood floor. She pushed up the sash and breathed the cold air. The palest of light out there. A storybook sky full of stars diffused by a high mist. After a while her heart calmed and then she could hear the ocean and the wind in the trees, and the dream let go of her.

She sat down on the chair and reached for her boots and pulled them on. The right boot always the reminder, always that. She tied the laces, and then in her hat and with her street coat over her nightgown she stepped out onto the landing and took the stairs down. In the thin white light from the sky and the yellow from the streetlamps she crossed the square to the church and at the side entrance used the key the priest had given her. She stepped inside. So quiet and dark at this hour. Only the eternal flame by the altar and the street-side windows gave some light.

She found her way to a front pew and sat there with her hands in her coat pockets. She looked at the piano, at the fine shape of it, the classic footed legs and the delicate prop stick, and in her mind she could see each part of it, the cabinet pieces still raw from the milling floor, the keyboard and its nerve endings, the fine soundboard with the bridge applied. The harp so heavy it took two men to raise it and four to set it into its lockpoints.

She stood up and walked to the place on the stone crossing where she thought the piano should be, and she looked up and clapped her hands and listened. She moved six paces to her left, closer to the wall, and clapped again.

On the way back to the hotel she looked in on her car. All was well. Frozen mist on the windows. She patted it on the fender and moved on. Up in the room she took off the coat and boots and hat and crawled back into bed.

A few hours later she sat in the dining room eating break-fast. Mildred came with a coffee mug from the kitchen and stood by her table.

"Mind if I join you?"

"Not at all. Please do."

"That was so very good last night. Honest. I sing in the choir, and so I know a bit about it. We're all familiar with the Navy Hymn, of course, but never like that. Not played like a straightforward melody but like a long ballad to draw you in and move you, and in a good way, like from someone really understanding you. I mean that. That's how it felt. So fine. Did you just improvise that?"

"Yes, I did."

"And the other piece, what was that?"

"That was something from the Brahms requiem. Father William let me choose it."

"It was good too. But what you did with the Navy Hymn . . . I feel like thanking you. I really do. *Thank you.*"

Mildred looked suddenly embarrassed, and she raised her coffee mug to cover the moment and took a sip and swallowed.

There was a pause and then Mildred said, "I almost forgot. Morris, that's the sexton, he was here before you came down. He said to tell you that Father William has invited you to walk in the funeral. You can come with me if you like, and I'll tell you a bit about this place."

The funeral was at ten. Crossing the square to the church she noticed Mildred's shoes, the good stitching and supple leather. She said so, and Mildred told her they'd been made by a man in town. Then they stood in the weak sunlight and more and more people came, dressed in black, all of them: men, women, and children. The boys had their hair combed with water, and their ears stuck out red in the cold. The girls had fresh ringlet curls, and some of them had little wreaths on their heads, small white paper blossoms that according to Mildred they'd later throw from the government dock to float out and bring comfort to the souls of the two men who had not been found. A few days earlier the Coast Guard had abandoned the search and had officially declared them lost and perished at sea.

"Very old words those are along here," said Mildred. "'Lost and perished at sea.' Old and much too common. I should know."

The coffin of shaved pine sat on trestles in the sun, and after the priest had blessed it, five fishermen and a Royal Canadian Mounted Policeman in his dress uniform shouldered it and carried it up the hill to the graveyard. Wives and mothers walked behind the ministrant, who carried the cross while Father William in a white surplice kept waving the censer. Wisps of smoke hung in the air, and the people behind them walked through it and some of them wept. The grass was bent and frozen where it was in the shade. Hoarfrost clung to the wire fence and sat on old crosses of carved stone. Madame Cabayé had talked about the historic cemetery. Acadians, mostly, she'd said. People who'd been deported or driven out, and many had moved south to Louisiana when it was still French and years later had come back from all over. They'd signed the British oath and settled here and then died in this place. And today three more crosses: two temporary ones out of barnwood at the memorial site, and one at an open grave.

When the coffin was at rest on the two boards across the hole, the priest handed the censer chains to the ministrant, and he folded his hands and raised his face to the sky. They stood for a moment while all was silent, and then in a voice so strong it made everyone look away from the coffin and up at this young priest of theirs, he called out:

> *Most Holy Spirit, who didst brood upon*
> *the chaos dark and rude*
> *And bid its angry tumult cease, and give,*
> *for wild confusion, peace,*
> *O hear us when we cry to thee*
> *for those in peril on the sea.*

———

Later he saw her walking past the open vestry door and he called to her: "Mrs. Giroux! A quick word if I may."

He stood up and waited for her before he sat down again. "You played very well last night. Thank you. A number of people have spoken to me about it. Some that used to sing in the choir."

"The acoustics in the church are good, Father. All that stone with just enough wood to soften the sound. I'd suggest moving the piano a bit. Closer to that curved wooden wall. It'll sound even better there."

"If you say so. Morris can do that. It's on casters and there's certainly enough room. I don't know when the organ will be fixed. It's an old McAllister. The parts have to be custom-made and then shipped from Boston, or maybe even from Edinburgh. That's expensive, and this church is poor like all of the French Shore and all of Nova Scotia. Things turned bad here in '27 and '28, not as bad as in Ontario, mind you, because they relied on industry. And then the stock market crash, of course. But our people here never had much money to invest, and now we still have the fishing and the agriculture. Most of our food is homegrown or it comes from the Annapolis Valley. Good soil and water there. We are fortunate in that."

"Yes. About the organ, now, Father. The old McAllisters have wonderful bronze pipes, but some of the workings are delicate. I happen to know that because we made linkages for them. In your organ, some parts will have been replaced more than once already."

"Yes, they have, according to the log. But it's getting ever more expensive. David Chandler thinks he might try and make them in his pattern shop. He says we could use heavy sailcloth for the bellows. David's a fine craftsman. Have you met him?"

"No. Not yet. But I've heard of him. He does leatherwork too, I'm told."

"Yes, he does."

Father William wore a black soutane with the Roman collar undone and the sleeves pushed up to his elbows. He had reddish hair cut short, red bristling eyebrows, and clear grey eyes filled with a young man's hope and trust. He might not be thirty yet, young enough to be her son. He sat studying her, taking his time with his hands folded on the table. Eventually he said, "Did Sidonie or Mildred tell you anything about us here?"

"A bit, yes."

"Saint Homais used to be all French, of course, just like the other stretches of the Shore, all the way around the turn past Yarmouth to places like Port L'Hebert and Port Joli, and even past that. Now the French are down to perhaps sixty per cent, but many of those are originals, like the Chouinards and the Cabayés and the Bissonnettes. Their names are on some of the oldest stones on the hill, and there's pride in that. But there are also many non-French that are from here, like Mildred, and many come-from-aways such as myself and David Chandler, who is an American. It's a close community, not unlike a large and sometimes quarrelsome family. My point is that, since the funeral, people have been asking me who you are and what brings you here and if you'll be staying."

"Well, I hope to be staying. But when you speak of the community, there is something I should tell you. I want to make it quite clear that my family was not exactly the churchgoing kind. Especially not after the Colonial Office blamed the missionaries for my father's death. I don't think my mother ever set foot in a church again."

"Your father was a missionary?"

"No. He was an engineer. In French West Africa, mostly."

"I see. But you are able to play the sacred repertoire? From the seventeen and eighteen hundreds?"

"Yes, of course. It's some of the most profound music we have. You heard me play the Brahms."

"Yes, I did. It was good. Now, when it comes to being *churchgoing*, as you put it, let me assure you that you won't be the only one in the community or even in the congregation that's uncommitted."

"Uncommitted?"

"Yes. Your faith. I understand, and I don't mind. Well, I do and I don't, because there's always hope. I *do* mind when they call themselves freethinkers, because thinking has nothing to do with it. The real freethinkers actually had the discipline to think in straight lines. Kierkegaard, Nietzsche. Martin Buber, who's still alive and still a sharp thorn in the side of the church. We studied them at the seminary."

He paused and looked down at his hands on the table. He looked up again. "This church used to be a cathedral," he said. "Do you know what that is?"

She felt herself blush. "A cathedral. Well, yes. I do know *that* much, Father. It's the main church in a diocese. Or the bishop's seat. Is there a bishop here?"

"Not any more. But this church is still the heart of our community, and it has a long history. It was consecrated a cathedral two hundred years ago, before the diocesan boundaries were redrawn. It will always be a cathedral in spirit, if not in practice. It was a community effort at the time, with all the locals pitching in and one master builder, a French architect, to guide them. Two men fell to their deaths building it. They are buried on the hill."

"It's beautiful," she said. "All that stone and the hand-squared beams and wooden ceilings. All that joinery, like upside-down ships."

"Yes, it's beautiful. Mrs. Giroux, I'll come right out with it. It's not just the organ – it's the choir, too. I don't think I mentioned that when we first spoke, before you auditioned. The thing is, I also need help with rebuilding the choir, but I wanted them to hear you first. Now that they've done that, I know they'll accept you. Some have spoken to me already."

"Yes. I would be glad to help with that. Very glad. What happened to the choir?"

"The usual. Jealousies and strife ever since Adelaide died a few months ago. She was our organist and conductor. We've been improvising ever since, and it's not going well. But a congregation needs good music. It brings them together."

"Well, I'd be glad to help, Father. Thank you for asking."

"Good. Very good." He stood up. "If you'd come with me to the office for a moment. The heating there is broken, and we don't use the room except for the telephone and the filing cabinet. I'll give you the choir list."

He led the way down the hall, and in the office he closed the door behind her. He went to the filing cabinet and pulled out a drawer, but then he paused for a moment. He turned to her.

"Mrs. Giroux, please forgive me. There isn't perhaps something more I should know about you? Before we go much further? Anything to prevent you from becoming active in our church?"

"I don't think so, Father. Other than what I told you."

"No? All right. Very well."

He turned and lifted out a file folder. "This is a list of the former choir members. Maybe Mildred can help with that, making the introductions. She's been active in the choir, and if she's not too busy I think she'll take the time. A rough diamond, our Mildred. One who speaks her mind, but a good, strong, honest person in the community, and a fine singing voice, as you'll see."

In her room she locked the door and then lay back on the bed with her boots on a towel. She could hear the ocean, wind in the trees. She sat up and undid the laces, hook by hook down to the eyelets, and took off the boots and set them on the floor and lay back again with her feet under the towel now.

The room was clean and bare, and every single thing she owned except for her nightgown and toiletries and street coat was still packed away. Two hat boxes, one suitcase, one leather-and-wood trunk. The trunk sat with the lid open against the wall. Each evening she hung up the day's clothes to air them, and she took out only what she would need the next day. In the morning she brushed the previous day's clothes, folded them and put them away.

She lay on the bed with her hands on her stomach. Long hands and strong piano fingers with the nails kept short. She could feel her hip bones under her wrists, too close to the surface because she'd become thinner these past few years; thinner and wiser and able to endure solitude absolutely. She lay still, with her eyes closed.

Ever since the accident she had not been sleeping well. After the jail and the institution she'd taken to sipping a brown medicine given to her by a pharmacist in Montreal, but it had not helped with the dreams and had kept her groggy all the next day and wanting ever more of it, and so by an act of will she'd stopped. She found it was better simply to submit and lie quietly in the dark and wait for sleep.

She rose and stepped to the window. The tide was halfway, coming in or going out she could not tell. She saw a brown shore, seaweed and enormous rocks exposed.

A sailboat was rounding a distant point of land. More rocks and evergreens, with mist low among them.

She heard the church bell and counted twelve strokes. Noon. *Maybe this place*, she said to herself. *Saint Homais*.

Three

THEY WERE NINE WOMEN and five men in Lady Ashley's living room, all in good clothes and the women with their hair nicely done. Mildred made the introductions. An upright piano stood against one wall – an English Broadwood in an oak cabinet – and Lady Ashley asked her to play something, to get things going.

She sat down, raised the fallboard and warmed up with a few chords and then played a bit of the Huron Carol, "'Twas in the Moon of Wintertime." After a few phrases she went back to the beginning and looked over her shoulder and nodded at them to sing. Several knew the work, but one voice overpowered the rest. She glanced back over her shoulder and saw that it was Lady Ashley. She kept playing, and when she could free her left hand for a moment she gave the downward *sotto* sign. It still wasn't very good, and she stopped and turned around. "We can work on that one," she said.

Lady Ashley rang a hand bell, and a young maid in a

black dress and white pinafore brought tea and plates of small sandwiches from the kitchen.

They all helped themselves, and she sat on the sofa and answered their questions. She told them she'd been wanting to move away from the big city, from Montreal, for some time. Her husband had been killed early in the war in France. She'd lived in England and then in Canada the last dozen years. In Montreal she'd met Madame Sidonie Cabayé, who'd told her about the French Shore and Saint Homais.

Everyone smiled and nodded. They remembered Sidonie.

And yes, she told them: she had a daughter who had gone to school in Montreal and was at this time taking a radiology course for registered nurses in London.

"Claire is twenty-four," she said. She searched her purse for the small leather folder with the photograph, and they studied it and passed it around and made comments about the grown daughter, one with a good profession in these times when even men had difficulty finding work.

At one point Lady Ashley rose abruptly and with a firm step left the room. Sir Anthony was in England on business, someone whispered. Wasn't he always, whispered someone else.

That night it snowed, and it kept on snowing until the middle of the next day. A very early snow, everyone said. Father William saw her struggling with the car, and he and the sexton came with shovels to help. The RCMP sergeant saw them from the road, and he parked his Ford and came to help also.

When the snow was cleared away from the wheels, she pulled out the choke and pumped the gas pedal and pushed the starter button. The engine hesitated but eventually it came to life, and the men slapped at the smoke and dropped the shovels and pushed. From the road she caught a glimpse of them in the mirror. The sexton and Father William were already walking away, but the policeman still stood looking after the car in a way she did not like. But the road was slippery and she had to pay attention, and the next time she checked the mirror he had turned away.

The snowplow had been through and she drove in second gear, with the worn-out pair of shoes on the passenger seat, past the school and the co-operative, past the government dock and on through a stand of pines to the building with the tall brick chimney.

In the front office she asked the girl if she could speak to Mr. David Chandler.

"You're the piano player, ma'am," said the girl brightly. "From the funeral. I recognize you. If you ever . . ." She blushed and stopped.

The girl was pretty in a way but there was something not quite right about one side of her face.

"If I ever what?" said Hélène.

"Oh, nothing, ma'am. You just go back out that door and turn left and you'll see the sign down the brickway. That's David's shop. You can go right in, but maybe cover your ears. It's often noisy in there with all that screamin' machinery he's got."

When she entered the shop he was standing at a sander, holding a workpiece to the belt with both hands. The dust that came off disappeared into the open mouth of the kind of suction machine that might have saved her mother's life, had there been one at the Molnar works. Around the room stood drawing boards and machinery and work tables. Hand tools hung within their outlines on pegboards. The workshop smelled of dry shaved wood, and for a moment it all took her back twenty years and more.

She walked between him and the window, and he looked up and nodded but kept on working. After a while he held up the piece and put callipers to it. He turned off the sander and the suction machine.

"Snow so soon," he said. He glanced at her city coat and hat and the shoes she was carrying. "How can I help you, ma'am?"

She said she was new in town but that she'd heard from Mildred at the hotel that he'd made her favourite pair of shoes.

"Her favourite pair," he said. "That's nice to hear."

She told him what she wanted, and he took the shoes and turned them in the light of the lamp over the work table.

"I can do that," he said. "If you sit in that chair and take off your boots, I can measure you for the last. Just have a seat while I wash up."

He went out through a door at the back of the room,

and she could hear water running. When he came back she was still standing.

"Could you not measure from the shoes, Mr. Chandler?"

"From the shoes. Well. It'll be so much better from the foot. Always from the foot, because every foot is different in small but important ways. Like the insteps or the arches, and how much the foot widens when we put weight on it. And so for the shoe to fit properly, that's how it's done."

He turned her right shoe in the light and put his hand inside.

"With this, all the more," he said.

She sat down on a bench.

"Ma'am?"

"Yes, Mr. Chandler. Just give me a moment." She looked around. "I spent most of my youth in a place like this. Much larger and more work stations, but the same wood smell and similar tools. My mother inherited a piano factory and she taught me the business. After she died I ran it for as long as I could. The war put an end to it."

He stood listening to her. Waiting, she imagined, for her to come to the point.

"Interesting," he said then. "And where was that?"

"In a town in northern France. Our make was called Molnar. We sent many to North America."

"Molnar pianos?"

"Yes. You have one right here in your church. I played it the night before the funeral."

"That was you? I wasn't there, but I heard about it."

She smiled at him. "Mr. Chandler," she said, "this shoe business is my secret."

"Well, ma'am. Your secret is safe with me."

"Thank you. Besides the pair to replace these, I need two pairs of indoor shoes. An elegant pair with a very low heel, almost flat, for recitals, and one with a slightly higher heel for other occasions. All black. Would you be able to do that?"

"Once I have a last, I can make any kind of shoe you want. Ankle boots, half-shoes. The heels, certainly."

He stood and waited. She sensed a firm kindness in the man, a courtesy and patience that made room for her concerns but also offered professional guidance.

"Mr. Chandler," she said. "One day, will you show me how this suction machine works? Where does the dust go?"

"Ah. It goes into a canvas bag in the basement just under here." He tapped his foot on the floor. "Once a month or so I have it emptied. I keep another shop for the leatherwork, in case you're wondering. This shop is for engineered patterns and other woodwork."

"Interesting," she said.

She took off her hat and put it beside her on the bench, and when she could postpone it no longer she set the left foot first on a wooden box there and leaned forward and began to undo the laces.

four

THE LAST PHOTO OF HER father had come from West Africa. His face looked tanned and there were hardly any wrinkles on it, just on his brow and at either side of his mouth. His laughing wrinkles, Mother called them. In the picture he wore a tropical shirt with the sleeves rolled up, and he stood holding up a tall wooden blade for the sort of windmill he designed and installed for water and electricity in the colonies. The main building of Habitation Midi, with five grinning black faces on the veranda, was behind him.

When the picture had first arrived in a letter, she'd sat studying it in the light of her desk lamp, and she imagined him speaking to the people behind him and joking with them. She imagined them all laughing and being grateful for his windmills and water pumps. These people and others in those faraway places saw much more of him than she did, and she envied them.

The day the news came to Montmagny, she was in the yard helping the workers load kiln-dried wood onto the cart that would take it to the milling floor. It was summer and she had on her pale-green printed dress and long leather work gloves because of the slivers.

A black motorcar arrived, and the driver stopped in the factory yard and shut down the engine. She watched a man get out on the passenger side and put on his hat and pull down his waistcoat.

"Where can I find Madame Bouchardon?" he said to no one in particular, and she turned and pointed at the wooden door across the yard.

The man walked there, and before he knocked he took off his hat and held it strangely close to his chest as though trapping a bird in it. He closed the door behind him, and within seconds she could hear her mother. The first scream was so loud that all the ducks flew off the millpond.

Mother's older cousin, Juliette, came over, and while Mother was resting after taking the nerve medicine Dr. Menasse had given her, Juliette told Hélène that her father had been killed in Africa, in Côte d'Ivoire. There had been some trouble, the man from the Colonial Office had said, some sort of tribal uprising to do with tithes imposed by missionaries, and all of Habitation Midi had been destroyed and every living thing there killed. Even the dogs.

Juliette paused and dabbed her eyes. She said, "I'm sorry, sweetheart. He was a good man, and he loved you and your mother very much. You must never forget that."

"The missionaries?" she said. "But why? What did anyone do to them?"

"No one did anything to the missionaries, Hélène. And your father did nothing to anyone."

"Was it the people on the veranda?"

"The what, dear?"

"On the veranda behind him. In the photograph."

"Oh, them. I don't think so."

"He was making windmills for them."

"I know."

There was a long silence.

"I know he was often away," said Juliette. "But not because he didn't want to be with you or with your mother. It was his work. He would have loved to be with you. He was a good father to you and a good husband to your mother, and he was a successful engineer. Remember those things as time goes by. Let no one take them from you. It's important."

But the fact that her father was truly gone and would never come back, not even for a short time between postings, did not sink in for a long time. After the news from Africa there were nights when he sat calmly by her bedside or when she could hear his voice in dreams, and she would feel safe and sleep on. She would tell Mother in the morning, and Mother would look at her across the breakfast table, pale and still, and not say anything.

———

Dr. Menasse told Juliette that Mother was exhausted. She needed rest, he said.

Hélène heard them through the closed library door because she was standing on the other side with her ear pressed to a glass against the wood.

"She works long hours and she's always worried," Juliette was saying. "It's not just her husband's death, it's also the business. There is so much competition and some of them make terribly good pianos, in modern facilities. She doesn't have the money to modernize, but even if she did, she's stubborn about doing things her way. The quality is wonderful, of course. Everyone says that, but at what expense?"

It was well known in the industry that with the help of modern machinery, firms like Bechstein and Bösendorfer could put out a piano every ninth day, while the Molnar factory was still mostly water-powered and pianos were made by hand, much the way they'd been since the beginning in 1850. A Molnar concert grand could take a month from start to finish, and a baby grand took not much less.

"Well," said Dr. Menasse, "I don't think there is too much wrong with her physically. Nothing that rest and good food won't cure. There is lots of room in this house, Juliette. Perhaps you could move in and lend a hand. You are family, after all."

"But I like it at the squire's lodge, Charles. I waited a long time for that apartment and I wouldn't want to give it up. At my age."

"I understand that. Hmm. What can I say? And you? Let me see your eyes and take your pulse."

There was silence for a moment in the library and then Dr. Menasse said, "Good, good." Hélène heard the snap of his doctor's bag.

"I suppose I could come in the mornings," said Juliette then. "Help out in the household. See how that goes."

"Yes," said Dr. Menasse. "You could try it."

Not very long after that, Nathan Homewood came knocking on the office door. He said he owned an export agency that sought quality instruments for America and Canada.

"May I?" he said, and pointed at a chair. "I have an important proposal for you."

He said there was a buyer from a large Boston firm visiting Paris right now, and he would like to bring the man here and make a presentation. The first order would probably be for no fewer than ten pianos. He repeated that for emphasis. *Ten pianos.* For a commission he wanted fifty per cent of net profits.

"Fifty per cent?" Mother said to her. "Is he mad? Did I hear that right?"

"Yes, Maman. Of net profits, not the gross."

"He can't be serious. Tell him that is impossible. It is ridiculous."

"Madame," said Nathan, "my French may not be perfect, but I think you can understand me without your lovely daughter's help. I agree that under normal circumstances one-half would be too much, but in this case I am opening up a very large and desirable market for you. Which would then be all yours."

Mother said she'd think about it.

"But what is there to think about, Madame? One-half of profits after all overhead and expenses. It will leave you with the other half free and clear in the bank. Business that you won't have unless I bring it to you. I repeat: What is there to think about? Tell me and I'll examine it with you."

Hélène sat watching him: the spark in his eye, the American self-assurance that would be considered immodest in a Frenchman. But it worked for Nathan. He was a nice-looking man with a good haircut, wearing a good suit and shined shoes, and his firm and reasonable way of speaking gave the listener confidence. She had never met anyone like him. So bold. So effective.

"I prepare my business ventures very carefully," he once told her, later. "So carefully that if someone says no to me, it must be because they haven't understood. And so I need to slow down and explain better. It's that simple."

On that first day he said to Mother, "Madame, let me point out that a deal like this will set you up in North America. It will spread the Molnar name in the right circles, and any further business over there will be yours, free and clear. All that in exchange for half the profit from just the initial transaction."

"Why Molnar?" said Mother. "I imagine that Bechstein

already has representation over there, but have you spoken to Bösendorfer or to Gaveau?"

"Of course I have. Would you rather I took my business to them?"

"No. But why Molnar?"

"Because I like what the music world says about the quality of your pianos. That they are exceptional. And also because I'm certain that since you are smaller, and you need to compete, you'll try harder than any of the other firms. Am I right, Madame?"

When the Boston buyer came, Mother, in a new skirt and blouse, showed him to the listening chair in the showroom, and Juliette served him hazelnut-cream biscuits and a good local Calvados. Mother took her place on the sofa and Nathan sat in a chair, further back. She herself had on a new sky-blue dress from Mouchaire, low-cut and taken in by Juliette to fit closely. She wore a thin gold chain around her neck, and her hair was brushed to a shine and held up with combs and a blue ribbon. On her feet she wore new kid slippers, the soles roughed with sandpaper for a good grip on the pedals.

She played the Liszt *Liebestraum*, and then she played some late Schubert and Schumann and Mozart.

By then she understood very well the importance of the first few notes – the power of good notes confidently played, with much of the music in the tension between them – and she demonstrated the grand, the baby grand, and the upright with all the skill and art she could muster.

The American buyer sat still and attentive. After the presentation of each model he shifted in his chair and nodded approval, and at the end he stood up and applauded.

"Bravo," he said. "Yes, indeed. Excellent."

The first order was for twelve pianos to be crated and shipped to Boston, and another six to Toronto. Never in the history of Molnar had there been an order anywhere near as large.

five

BY THE MIDDLE OF HER sixth day in Saint Homais she'd already worked twice with the choir. The piano was slightly out of tune, and that afternoon she used the 5/16-inch wrench she'd borrowed from David Chandler and tuned it. Before the war, whenever they had shipped a Molnar to America or to an English colony, they had sent along a six-millimetre pin wrench. Morris hadn't been able to find the one that had come with this piano, and so she had asked David Chandler to cut her a thin metal shim to use with the wrench. She started with the one tuning fork she still owned, an A440, and then worked her way up and down through the strings by ear and intuition.

Near the end Mildred came and sat in a front pew. "How on earth do you do that?" she said when Hélène had finished.

"I had two very good teachers. My mother had perfect pitch – *l'oreille absolue*, it's called. It made her an excellent tuner, just as good as some of the blind ones. Especially in the final stages, the last tiny adjustments to strings and sometimes even to links and dampers that some call voicing. I learned from her and from our master installer. He used to say, *Rounded shoulders to the notes, Mademoiselle. Perfect in the middle, but rounded sides, nothing abrupt.* How often did I hear him remind me of that?"

They were sitting side by side in the front pew. Morris walked past, and he nodded at them and kept going. Somewhere a door opened and closed.

"I just had a run-in with Lady Ashley," said Mildred. "My, how that woman can be difficult."

"What happened?"

"She says she may stop singing in the choir."

"Oh? Why?"

"I think she was hoping to lead it, but then Father put you in charge. It was the right thing to do even though you're from away, but she doesn't like it."

"Should I talk to her?"

"I'd wait a bit, see what she does. I know she didn't like you shushing her with the Huron Carol, but she and Adelaide didn't get along either."

"I wasn't *shushing* her, Mildred. I gave her the down sign. There's a difference. If she wants to sing in a choir, she'll have to get used to taking directions."

"Oh, I know. I didn't mean anything. But she's ambitious. We all know that."

They sat in silence for a moment and then Hélène said, "I called my daughter this morning, in London. Maybe she'll come over for Christmas. Right now she's preparing for an exam."

"A fine profession, that," said Mildred. "Nursing. I'd have liked to do something like that. But then I met my husband, and he was a cook. They'd sent him to Montreal to a chef school and I learned from him. I was a McTaft before my marriage, have I told you that? His mother, old Madame Yamoussouke, left him the hotel. It was a bit run-down, but we built it up with just very good food. Made our name with that, and then he died on me. When we had the flu here, after the war. Only thirty-six, he was."

"Much too young. I'm sorry."

Morris came back into the sanctuary. He was carrying a long-handled plume, and he reached up with it and began dusting the light fixtures that hung from the crossbeams.

Hélène said, "Father William showed me the little apartment up in the annex. I think I'll take it."

"I'm not surprised. If you're going to stay here, you need a place of your own. His cook used to live there, before she got married. It's nice, if you don't mind the steep stairs."

"I'll get used to them. And there's a handrail. I love the views from up there. And I can still have my meals at the hotel."

"I hope so! We can set up an account if you like, and you just pay me once a month."

~

At the end of her last year in primary school, the Molnar master installer began to teach her about pianos. Monsieur Bendix Raoul was not from the area; he came from what he called "real hammer mill country" in the French Alps, valleys of knife makers and gunsmiths and tool makers, plant after plant powered by the same river, and during his journeyman years he'd travelled widely and worked his way up through the strict guild system. He had grey hair and careful hands, and he always wore a faded blue shop coat with dusty reading glasses in the breast pocket. He never rushed anything, and from him she learned step by step over the years how to work with tuning fork and pin wrench and the raw keyboard; how to pay close attention to each of the many moving parts that connected a key to the hammer that would then touch the strings. She watched his fingers on the keys, firm yet gentle, his head bent and slightly turned to the side. Striking a key five, six times, and then just once more, and already knowing by how much to adjust each string.

From him she learned how to be precise and methodical, and from him she accepted what too often she rebelled against when it came from her mother.

"You know by now that a piano has many more strings than keys, Mademoiselle," he said to her one day in the stillness of the cork-lined room. "The ratio depends on the model, of course, but let's take our grand piano, for example. Two hundred and eight strings to eighty-eight keys. Many more hammers touch strings in threes and twos than in singles. So the question is, to what degree should the side strings resonate differently from the main? You see, that is the art in the craft. The human ear wants to hear not just one isolated note at a time. It wants soft edges, a touch of polyphony. And it does not want to just *hear* that note, Mademoiselle. It wants to *feel* it."

She was ten years old then. She'd been taking piano at the conservatory since the age of six, and now began her formal apprenticeship in the serious business of piano making.

Monsieur Bendix Raoul, because she liked and trusted him, had also been the one finally able to convince her that a dog on the factory grounds was not a good idea. Her mother had been saying that all along and there had been fights and tears over it, but when Bendix Raoul eventually talked to her about it, she came around. It helped that he made her see it from the dog's point of view.

"Mademoiselle," he said to her, "a dog can be an affectionate and loyal companion, I grant you that. But you won't always be there to watch out for it."

"Why not? I would be very responsible."

"I'm sure you would be. But what about when you are at school, for instance? Or in the house, and the dog is out here? And how would you feel if some injury were to happen to the dog? This is a factory."

"I would train it. Dogs are intelligent."

"Yes. Some are. But I once knew a dog at a factory down south and it got caught in the master belt from the mill shaft, Mademoiselle. That's the widest belt on the floor and it's often loose like ours is, and that dog got caught in it and the belt carried it into the cogs and right around and up through the idler. It was terrible, Mademoiselle. All the fur and skin was torn off and when they finally got to it—"

She covered her ears and told him to stop. "Is that true?" she said.

He nodded. "It was terrible."

"I could have a long leash and tie it up when I'm not here."

"Yes, you could do that. But think about it. Imagine you are the dog, and how would you like being tied up for hours? And all the noise and goings-on around you. The saws and routers and the trucks coming and going."

This conversation took place under a grand piano, when they both were on hands and knees so that he could point out to her the principles of soundboard anchoring and the subtle thinning and widening of the frame.

He said, "Maybe take your time and think about it, Mademoiselle. Look around at all the dangers here on the floors and in the yard. For the men too, when they're carrying cabinet pieces. But think of the dog, mostly."

She did think about it, and eventually there was no more talk of a dog.

Six

NATHAN HOMEWOOD came more than ten years later, and the way her entanglement and her problems with him began was strange and quick and wholly unexpected.

The Boston order had essentially saved the company and, as a result, Nathan became a frequent visitor and dinner guest at the house. On the third such evening he brought twenty long-stemmed roses, and he grinned with his usual confidence and handed them to her.

Mother and Juliette exchanged glances but made no comment. By the end of that dinner they were treating him like a family friend. They called him *Monsieur Ohm-bois*, and he enjoyed that. Her, he called Miss Helen, and then just Helen. He said the first-name basis was the American way and that the proper pronunciation of those accented vowels defeated him.

He told them his family had been Americans who'd moved north to Canada, and then some had gone back. His parents had moved to New Mexico for the climate, and he was now dividing his time between England and the Continent and North America, always on the lookout for new business opportunities.

Before long it became her task after those visits to see him out, to turn on the lights on the stairway and to walk down with him and then to unlock the front door. Mother's design, of course, to give them moments of privacy. Saying goodbye, he would stand close, holding her hands, and kiss her on both cheeks, on the left and then the right, and his lips would try to linger there. The first few times, she held still while she considered this. It was confusing. Even though she found him interesting in some way, these moments made it clear to her that he was not a man she would choose for herself – perhaps as a man to learn from, but not as a future husband or even as a lover. She was not sure why, and was not interested in analyzing it.

"Mother," she said firmly after the third or fourth such occasion, "from now on would you mind walking him down yourself? I don't want to. And will you please stop encouraging him. I'm not interested in him that way."

"You are not? Why on earth not?"

They were standing in the hallway between dining room and kitchen, and Mother was carrying a tray of used dishes.

"I don't know," said Hélène. "And it doesn't matter. Here. Let me take that."

"Dear child," said her mother. "I'm just so astonished. I thought you were interested. All those roses. And he's a good-looking man, a talented businessman, and one day he'll be rich, if he isn't already. Maybe give it time."

"I don't think that's how it works," said Hélène. "Giving it time. One either knows or one doesn't. And can I decide that for myself?"

Minutes later she overheard Mother and Juliette in the kitchen, and Juliette was saying, "You don't know better than the girl. Just because he brought business and *you* like him doesn't mean she has to as well. Maybe you just feel indebted to him. Is that it?"

"Don't be silly. He seems like a good choice. He's clever and decisive. I can say that much, can't I? And good-looking. Mothers have a certain right when it comes to things like that. An obligation, even. Don't interfere in this, Juliette."

"I am not. I'm talking to *you*, aren't I? Not to Hélène. But you must let her decide for herself. You did that, and where do you think she got her stubborn streak from?"

All these conflicts ended when she met Pierre; it was sudden and so very clear to her, and there was absolutely nothing to be done about it.

The first time she saw him was on the train coming home from the city after a day at the foundry that was making the harps and the bronze MOLNAR, FRANCE inlay for the fallboards. She had her music diploma by then, but not yet her trade permit or the guild brief. Mother insisted that she learn every aspect of the business, and the days at the foundry were meant to give her an appreciation of the engineering principles that went into the various cast-iron harps so that with a minimum of mass they could withstand the combined pull of a piano's steel strings, which added up to many thousands of pounds.

The first time she noticed him, she felt shy and would not look at him directly, but she kept glancing across the carriage aisle as if to see out the windows there, and when their eyes finally met as if by chance, he smiled. The next day she made sure to be on the same train, again in the second carriage, and he was there. This time he stood up and crossed over to her and introduced himself. His name was Lieutenant Pierre Giroux, and he was fresh from military college, posted as an adjutant to the garrison in the city. They met twice more on the train and then in Montmagny at Faustin for ice cream.

He had been born of French colonial parents in Dahomey, in French West Africa, not far from where her father had disappeared. In her school atlas Dahomey was just two centimetres over from Côte d'Ivoire. There had been other boyfriends – local boys and city boys to go to dances with and for walks – and most recently there'd been the annoyance with Nathan. But this new one, Pierre from Dahomey, was altogether different. He was sweet and thoughtful and he had brown eyes, and she loved his smile and the way he looked at her.

That day at Faustin they sat spooning ice cream and chatting so easily. He was in civilian clothes and his shirtsleeves were rolled up because it was a warm fall day. The leaves on the chestnut trees were turning and the sun came through them, golden and warm. She loved looking at him: at his face, the shape of his lips, his tanned hands. His smile.

This will never change, she said to herself. And at home in her room, at her desk in the light from the old paper lampshade with cut-out bears from her childhood, she wrote it down like a promise: *This will never change*.

It was still her secret then.

But Nathan kept coming to visit. Relentlessly so, it seemed to her. Once he even took a three-day holiday and stayed at the hotel in town. Twice he appeared unannounced at the factory to find her in her shop coat and with her hair full of sawdust, and he suggested a walk on the trundle path along the river.

The second time, in a fit of anger and to put an end to this, she agreed. It was a cool day, and she fetched her coat and a scarf and then led the way. They had not gone very far when she stopped and turned to him.

"Nathan," she said. "There is something I need to tell you."

"Oh, all right." He smiled at her. "What? Let me guess." He stood with his back half turned to the river and with one hand on the wooden railing.

She briefly touched that hand with hers. "No need to

guess, Nathan. You won't like this, but I am not free. There is someone else."

He stared at her. "What? But . . . I don't understand. Since when?"

"That doesn't matter. Listen, Nathan. There are many things I admire about you. Your business skills, your frankness. I've learned about that from you, and so I'm being frank also. I like you but not the way I need to like, never mind love, a future husband. You did a great service for Molnar, but you also benefitted handsomely from it as well. Can't I just like you as a friend? Someone to learn from. Isn't that also something?"

"Is it the difference in our ages? It's not that much. You are twenty-two and I am just thirteen years older. Or is it because I'm not French?"

"No, no. It's nothing that simple. Please don't ask me to explain. I couldn't anyway. It's how I feel."

"Who is it? What's his name?"

"That doesn't matter either. Please don't probe."

He said nothing for a while, and it was almost as if he'd suddenly shrunk in height, the way he turned to look at the water. She felt sorry for him. She felt guilty and she wanted this to be over with, said and done and forgiven.

She touched his hand once more.

"Nathan, you are an interesting man in so many ways. You are bold and clever, and Mother and Juliette think highly of you. You'll find someone else in no time. Of course you will. Nathan? Please."

"We shall see," he said then. He was still not looking at her. "Love can grow from friendship. I am not giving up hope. I can wait."

"*Wait*? Nathan, please don't even think that. I wouldn't like the feeling that you're standing back, *waiting* for me."

He said nothing for some time, and there was not one word that she could add to ease the tension. After a while he let go of the railing and started to walk away. "Come," he said over his shoulder. "I should let you get back to work."

For some minutes they walked in silence, then he said, "I'll be speaking to your mother about our business arrangement. Because of your antiquated methods, you are behind with the Boston order, you realize that. But I'll talk to them. I respect your decision, Helen. Thank you for telling me. It was fair and square, as we say in America. I won't be coming to the house socially any more."

When she told them, Mother was at first amazed, then she became upset, but eventually she accepted the situation. Both Mother and Juliette wanted to meet Pierre, and she was asked to invite him for dinner. He arrived in his dress uniform, and he bowed to the women and unclipped his sabre and put it in the umbrella stand in the hallway.

He had good table manners and lively conversation, and after a few such dinners Mother said that she might get to like him, that he appeared to be intelligent and cul-tured. It was too bad that he was a soldier, because soldiers had to go where the politicians sent them. These days that was the colonies, Mother said, and the colonies were far away. She looked straight at Hélène saying that. Then she repeated the words *far away*, and added, "Your father wasn't a soldier, but he too spent much more time in the colonies than he did here at home with us."

"I know, Maman. I do know that. We all do."

"And?"

"And nothing."

"Well," said Mother after a long pause. "I do like the way he looks at you. With his brown eyes."

Juliette approved of him too. She winked at Hélène and explained that what she liked most about him was that he had high expectations, not of others but of himself, of the kind of man he aimed to make of himself. She said he had *caractère*.

In those weeks and months she loved showing off her town to him: the streets that radiated out from the church square, lined by buildings seven and eight hundred years old, so ancient, all of it; the old museum and the new concert hall; the fountain where in the spring and fall a stage was erected for the travelling passion plays and morality plays, with electric lights on the backdrop of stone and tile roofs, the actors in medieval garb, the women in kirtles or gowns, the men in tunics and leggings and belts, their shouts echoing around the square, their boots loud on the stage planks, the shadow of a gallows never far away.

She showed him the river that still powered much of the town's industry, and where as children she and her friends had come flying down the rapids, screeching and laughing, clinging to improvised rafts.

One day when the mill downstream was cutting Molnar veneer, she took him there, and they stood and watched as steam hissed from nozzles and softened the wood, and sharp blades peeled off thin sheets of veneer, which were then rolled up and sealed in wax cloth to keep them flexible.

The logs that day were from precious fruit trees, plum and cherry and pear. They came from an exhausted orchard on the north side of the river. She leaned close to Pierre and told him over the noise that her maternal grandfather had bought the rights to the trees the day they were planted. That long ago.

She said that after the trees were cut, the bark was removed to prevent beetles, and then the logs were stored to cure for another ten years in a vented shed. Plenty of air was kept between them and they were turned every so often, like wine bottles, which was why the texture and the colours in the grain were so rich and even.

"Look at this one," she said. "It must be pear coming off the rollers now. Along with rosewood, pear is our most expensive veneer, and it's only used for inlay and borders. Remind me to show you the picture we have of the early days of the workshop. The entire assembly was still wood then. Imagine! Oak, usually, or walnut. And just hand tools and iron blades they used, Pierre. Carbon steel was already available, but even though rust was a problem they preferred iron because it's softer and you get a better edge. In fact, we still use iron blades for the fine work. Even now. They have edges so keen and flexible, they'll bend when you run them over your thumbnail. With them the men can make cuts so tight you can hardly see them . . ." She paused. "What are you smiling at?"

"You, Hélène. Your enthusiasm. Tell me more."

Two years after she met him, the generals sent Pierre to Rouen, and a year later to Paris. During that time she saw him only every other week, when he had a three-day pass, but it was always wonderful. By the time they sent him to Indochina, he was a major and she was happily married to him.

The Boston and Toronto consignments had long since been delivered and paid for, and Nathan had received his share along with a detailed accounting. He still wrote letters, but she never wrote back. How he knew of the wedding and later of Claire's birth he never said, but he sent presents, a cut-glass bowl from Prague for the wedding and then a music-box piano for Claire that, when opened, played "Für Elise." Juliette wrote the thank-you notes.

By then Hélène was finished with her training and ready for the final guild exam. As her work sample the board of examiners wanted a finished soundboard for a baby grand, with frame mounts and bridge indicated and all strings drawn precisely, all the strengths and angles and supports and pitch notes. She made it from five-centimetre strips of Norway spruce, glued and clamped and shaved to perfection and then marked up in pencil. It took five hours every evening for six weeks. On the day of the examination, two workers helped her load it onto a padded Molnar truck and strap it down and deliver it, and at its destination the men set it on the backs of four chairs. The examiners made her wait and watch while they murmured and scratched their beards and nodded wisely, and measured with parallel ruler and tong-calliper.

She wrote the exam for her trade permit, and when she passed, the lawyer, on Mother's instructions, entered her as *directrice* in the company documents.

The first grand piano she set up and then voiced all by herself in the cork-lined room was destined for a famous music school in New York. It was checked by Mother and then by Bendix Raoul, and they approved.

They stood and watched as she pressed her own small oval master stamp with the letters H.G. onto the transom. It was a rite of passage she would never forget.

Seven

ON THE MORNING OF the move from the hotel to the apartment, she put away her nightgown and her toiletries in the suitcase. She closed the lid and put the suitcase on top of the trunk and then sat on the bed with her hands in her lap. Her coat and hat lay ready by her side.

Out the window it was snowing again, snow that came down so thick she could not see past the trees. She could not see the ocean at all. The world might be ending at the trees.

She heard voices, and stood up and went to open the door. The men had snow on their shoulders and hats. They brought a smell of clean, cold air into the room. Father William asked if she was ready, and she stepped back and waved a hand at her luggage.

"Thank you both for doing this," she said. "I could carry one of the hat boxes. Or both."

"Oh, no," said Father William. "Not at all, Mrs. Giroux. Footing's poor out today. You'll be wanting to wear galoshes. Do you have any?"

They took the trunk first, each holding up one end by the leather handle.

"Maybe you go ahead, missus," said the sexton. "You can open the doors for Father and me."

Half an hour later it was all done, and she and Father William stood in her new home up the steep stairway at the back of the church. A coal fire was burning in the grate, and they could hear Morris in the bathroom trying the taps and the toilet and the hand shower.

She looked around: bedroom and living room, the furniture in reasonably good condition. Windows with views of the town and of trees and the Gulf of Maine. A small kitchen with a table and a three-ring burner. A larder set into the wall, with vent holes for outside air.

"What do you think, Mrs. Giroux?"

"Oh, I like it. I do."

"You might want to paint the bathroom ceiling. Morris could help with that."

"I'll see."

"Well, good, Mrs. Giroux. By the way, I have great hopes for our music program. And next year, maybe even for a music festival in the summer or fall. Have I mentioned that? It's been one of my hopes for some time now."

"No, you haven't. A music festival?"

"Yes. I feel sure that our town council would support it. And people would travel for that, bring money to the community. Americans would come across from New York and Maine. We could invite string players and some woodwinds for a few weeks in the season. Call it the French Shore Music Festival. That has a nice ring, doesn't it?"

Over the next few days, she opened an account at the Dominion Bank and had her money transferred from Montreal. She practised the piano and worked with the choir, and she emptied her suitcase and the trunk. Some of her clothes had lain folded in there for nearly three years, and she hung them in the closet to let the creases fall out.

She wanted a shelf for her few books and the framed photograph of Pierre, and she asked David Chandler if he could make one. Just three boards, she told him, and with her hands spread out she indicated how wide and how high. He brought it over the very next day and mounted it for her on the living room wall near the coal fire.

She told him it was beautiful. Clear pine, precisely fitted and pegged and varnished and mounted in a clever way, flush to the wall so that one could not see the hooks.

"Let me pay you now, Mr. Chandler," she said. "I never even asked about the price."

He laughed and said not to worry. It would not be much, and he'd combine it with the invoice for the shoes.

He looked around. "This is a nice place, Mrs. Giroux. And the views! I've never been up here."

"You must come for tea sometime. I'll have to go now and practise, but come tomorrow if you can. Around four?"

When he'd left she ran her hand over the shelf. She

touched the wood where the joints had to be, and they were so well made she could make them out only by the change in direction of the grain. Her very own piece of furniture, the first in years, and such good work.

That evening she sat eating dinner with Mildred at the hotel. They had not finished the soup when Morris arrived and said that Father William wished to speak with her.

"What, now?"

"Well, yes," said Morris. He stood by their table in a black coat with his hat in his hands.

Outside in the street she asked him if he knew what it was about, and he said he did not.

The RCMP Ford with chains on the rear wheels was parked by the side door, and when they reached the vestry the policeman and Father William pushed back their chairs and stood up. A closed file folder lay on the table under the policeman's hat.

Her heart was pounding.

"Thank you, Morris," said Father William. "Please close the door on your way out."

They sat down and Father William said to her, "Mrs. Giroux, you know our Sergeant Elliott. Halifax has forwarded a letter from the provincial court in Edmonton to his constabulary. He'll tell you what it's all about."

The sergeant opened the file folder and spread out its contents. Among the papers she saw two photographs of herself. One was from before the war, and it showed her in the fitted wool jacket with her hair still deep black. That picture had been in a magazine where they declared her to be the youngest woman manager of a company with more than fifteen employees in the whole of Artois province. It had been Pierre's favourite picture of her. He used to say he loved the proud tilt to her head and her full, kissable lips.

The other picture had been taken many years later by a press photographer at the back of the police station in Edmonton. She was walking on crutches next to a policeman, and her face was bruised and there was crusted blood on it. She wore no hat, and the combs had fallen out of her hair. Her eyes were round, and in them there was only terror. *Madness*, one newspaper had said.

Father William leaned forward to look at the pictures, and impulsively he covered his mouth with his hand and he looked at her and then quickly away.

The sergeant unfolded a piece of paper, and he put it down and smoothed it with his hand. It was typewritten and it had seals and looping signatures on it.

"Mrs. Hélène Giroux," he said. "You are Mrs. Hélène Giroux?"

"Yes."

"Please show me your driver's permit."

She found it in her purse and pushed it across the table. She did not look at Father William. She could not.

The sergeant studied the document and handed it back.

"Mrs. Giroux," he said. "I have here before me a warrant to give notice and to apprehend. You are to be held on fresh evidence relating to the unnatural death of Mr. Nathan Homewood in November 1929 in the province of Alberta." He pushed the piece of paper across the table towards her. "Do you understand? Please take a look."

"Don't say anything, Mrs. Giroux," said Father William. "The sergeant tells me there is no need to say anything now."

"Well, no, Father," said the sergeant. "Don't you be buttin' in, now. She needs to tell me if she understands the charge. I have to ask. It's a king's warrant."

He looked at her. "Do you understand the nature of this warrant, Mrs. Giroux?"

"Yes, I do."

She sat back in the chair with her head up and her lips pressed together. She fussed a handkerchief from her sleeve but then pushed it back firmly with thumb and forefinger. The men watched her. When she said no more, the sergeant reached for the warrant and put it among the other papers in the folder.

"Mrs. Giroux, a warrant to apprehend means I have to keep you in custody until the first hearing, but under the circumstances, which are that at the moment I have no separate cell and no matron to keep an eye on you, the Father here suggested house arrest. Which is in fact my other legal option. But it means you would have to agree to remain confined to these premises, the church and the annex attached to it. If you flee, we will find you and you'll be sent to the women's penitentiary in Dartmouth. Fleeing custody would be one more criminal charge against you. Do you understand that, and do you agree to abide by the terms of this arrest?"

She nodded, and he said, "I need to hear you say yes or no with good volume. Father William will be my witness that you have done so, and I will make a note in the file."

And she cleared her throat and said, "Yes. I do understand and I do agree."

"You see," said Father William when the policeman had left. "I had a feeling. I hoped I was wrong, but I had a feeling. A woman like you arriving here out of nowhere. You'll remember when I asked you if there was perhaps something more that I should know about you. And you said no."

"Because there wasn't anything more to tell. And certainly not *this*. Yes, there was a court case three years ago, but why should I have mentioned that when it was dismissed?"

"You might still have mentioned it."

"I did not see the need."

"You were wrong. The other day when we were giving you a push, the sergeant saw something about your licence plate that got his attention. Apparently Quebec has different date tabs now. You said you were from Montreal, and you don't know that? When were you last there?"

"Just before I came here. I had lived there for years and then in Moncton and other places, and most recently I spent a few more days in Montreal. That was when Madame Cabayé mentioned Saint Homais to me."

"I see. In any case the sergeant made inquiries, and that's how he learned that they were looking for you. Did you know that?"

"No, I did not. I had been accused of something, but I was acquitted."

"Accused of what?"

"Does it matter?"

"Accused of what, Mrs. Giroux? The warrant mentioned an unnatural death."

"Yes. I was charged in connection with that."

They sat in silence for a moment. The leaded window was dark with the night, and chalices and a glass beaker shone dimly on a stone ledge. Vestments with gold thread hung on a hook.

After a while Father William moved in his chair. "And who was Nathan Homewood?"

"A man I was travelling with. A friend and business partner."

"I see. Well, apparently some prosecutor has new evidence to do with his death. The sergeant couldn't say what."

"I had no idea. I need to call my daughter in London."

"You can do that from the church office. Mrs. Giroux, promise me that you won't step through any exterior door or even be seen in a door opening."

"I promise."

"Good. Use the phone in the morning. The long-distance exchange is closed now."

She looked into his eyes and they were sad. Worse, they were disappointed.

"There are explanations for all this," she said.

"Oh, I'm sure. But not tonight. If you would please go upstairs now. I am sorry it came to this. Did you finish dinner at the hotel?"

She shook her head.

"I could have something sent up."

"No. But thank you. Father William . . ."

He waited a moment, and when she said nothing more he stood up.

"Let's talk in the morning. We all need to calm down and reflect on this. Good night, Mrs. Giroux."

He held out his hand and she almost reached to shake it, but he said, "Your car keys, please."

The Long Road

Eight

NATHAN HOMEWOOD always kept in touch. Along the way he even sent two sales leads from Paris, and those deals did in fact close. He wrote that he did not want any commission, but Mother mailed him a cheque anyway, for the five per cent customary in the trade. He cashed it.

Letters from him kept arriving: from Canada, from England, from Egypt, from America. Sometimes a letter was addressed to her, sometimes to her mother. Her mother usually opened her mail at the breakfast table and then, often not wanting to bother with her glasses, handed the letters across the table for Hélène to read.

"He's in London now," she said one morning early in 1909. "Doing some kind of logistics work. He says it's about shipments from Canada to Britain. Listen to this: 'ships full of lumber and copper and gold and whatever else they can steal.'"

"*Steal,*" said Mother. "Is that what he says? The Americans may have shaken them off, but whether he likes it or not, English Canada is a British colony by whatever name. They took it and now it's theirs."

"I wish he'd stop writing."

"Does it really matter? He is not an unpleasant person, and he was very good for our business. We must always remember that."

"I think that the only reason he came to us with that deal was because he'd done his research, as he kept saying. He knew Molnar was in trouble and with us he could get the highest commission. Bösendorfer or Bechstein would have shown him the door."

"Maybe," said Mother. "But that is business. He is clever and he was right."

Ever since she'd told Dr. Menasse that she'd try to help, Juliette had been coming to the house in the mornings. She'd put on the white bib apron and lift the household keys from the hook in the kitchen and take charge. And because Juliette also helped out with Claire, both Hélène and her mother were able to concentrate fully on the factory. Mother offered to pay Juliette something to supplement her pension, and Juliette accepted.

When Claire was nearly two, they prepared to travel to Indochina in order to spend time with Pierre and to promote Molnar in the colony. Travel outfits were bought, and Mother had a baby grand crated for her to take along. Mother also designed a collapsible child carrier with an upright seat for quick transportation. She called it an *enfantmobile*, and the men on the shop floor made it from canvas and poplar and the wheels of an Oxford tea trolley. Before long Hélène kissed her mother and Juliette goodbye, and then she and Claire travelled by train to Marseilles and from there on the steamer *Patrie* south and through the Suez Canal into the Indian Ocean.

Weeks later, in Haiphong harbour, Pierre came out on the launch to meet them, and when she first saw him again, in his tropical uniform with his suntanned face and his eyes so happy, all she could do was laugh and weep at the same time. She stood at the portside rail holding up Claire, and Pierre's smiling face was all she could see, and Claire's hair, pure black like her own and freshly washed that morning, blew into her face and it was all she could feel and smell.

"*Chérie*," said Pierre, and he stroked her wet cheek and kissed her lips. He eased Claire from her arms and carried her on his shoulders as they walked down the gangway to the launch.

Haiphong was the main naval base for the French in Indochina. It was an old city of crowded streets and of some good restaurants and shops, of fine evening views of the Gulf of Tonkin to the east and of plantations all the way to the western horizon. Pierre was renting a small house on Tonkin Hill, and from its terrace one could see the sunrise over Hainan. Some mornings when Claire and Pierre were still asleep she would tiptoe out the sliding door in her nightgown and stand in the astonishing light of five a.m., when the ships in the harbour still lay in darkness, while above them the sun pushed forth like some molten thing breaching the earth's crust and up into the sky over the island, and instantly the day was hot.

On most Saturday evenings, she and two string players from the symphony orchestra gave recitals in the main concert hall. The baby grand had survived the journey well, but because of the high humidity it had to be tuned frequently, at times even during intermissions with the curtain drawn. The pin block was still a single piece of hardwood then, and it was during one of those tunings in Haiphong that she studied the anchoring of the block and then wrote to her mother suggesting that the block be made in segments as tight inserts into openings at the very base of the harp, and that metal should replace as much wood as possible. She sketched her idea on a separate page in the letter.

The cellist at her recitals was Madame Tran. She had studied at the Sorbonne and was not much older than Hélène. They became friends, and Madame Tran gave her lessons in Vietnamese. Claire always came along and afterward would amaze her parents with the Vietnamese words and phrases she remembered.

One day on their way home from a lesson, they discovered a park not far from the hill, and from then on the three of them would often go strolling there in the evenings, Pierre in his uniform and she and Claire in linen dresses and ribbon hats and white shoes. They walked past bushes pruned into the shapes of animals, and they would identify the animal and then ask someone the name in Vietnamese, and that person would stop and say the word and listen to them repeating it.

In that same park there was a wilderness area near a pond, and in that soil grew small magical wildflowers that kept their blossoms tightly closed during the day. So tight that barely a thickening showed at the end of the stem, but at night, in full darkness, the flowers opened to a deep red and purple, and they spread an aroma sweet and unusual like rare perfume. Tiny, colourful birds came to feed there in the dark, much smaller than a hummingbird, smaller than Claire's thumb. Twice she and Pierre and Claire brought a blanket and mosquito netting and a flashlight, and they lay on that blanket like children and watched the spectacle of the midnight flowers and the tiny birds.

When Pierre was not on field duty he could come home in the evenings, and there were stretches when for two weeks in a row they could spend every night together. She would always remember that: the lovely times in Haiphong when they could have dinners on their own terrace, and when she and Pierre could sleep in the same bed night after night, and lie in each other's arms and wake up together in the morning. They became a true family then, living together under the same roof, something they had rarely been able to do in France because of his postings and her obligations at the piano works.

But one morning she was summoned to the consulate and handed a radio telegram from Dr. Menasse. In it the doctor said that her mother had fallen ill and was asking her to come home.

She telephoned and spoke to Juliette and then to her mother, but Mother's voice was too weak for her to understand.

And so from one day to the next everything was different, and their magical time in the little house on Tonkin Hill was over.

In her year in Indochina she had sent home orders and down payments for seven pianos, among them two concert grands for the symphony orchestras in Haiphong and Hanoi. Now she sold the baby grand to the baker's wife and said goodbye to Madame Tran. They sat over orange tea, and when she left, Madame Tran embraced her the French way, and then she reached out and with one fine finger made a circle on Hélène's forehead.

Back at the house she packed her own and Claire's trunks. Pierre came along on the launch, and he held Claire's hand all the way across the harbour. When the launch slowed, he knelt on the deck and embraced Claire.

That single piercing image of Pierre kneeling and his face so sad would remain locked in her mind for years afterward, and at first whenever the image came to her it created terror and the fear of more loss, but after some time it brought only gratitude for what had been and was now hers in memory forever.

Nine

IN THE MORNING SHE sat on the chair by the telephone in the freezing church office and spoke to Claire in London.

"Oh, Mom," said Claire. "Give me the details. What the policeman said."

She told her. There was not much.

"New evidence. What new thing could they have dug up?"

"I have no idea. I was hoping you could come and visit, Claire. Are you finished with the exam?"

"I've done the practical. The written is tomorrow."

"Can you come then? Use the money in the special account. It's there for emergencies, and that's what this is now."

"I'll see what I can do. I'll talk to the head nurse."

She told Claire she loved her, and Claire said she loved her too. Claire said, "Don't worry, Mom. They dismissed it once, they'll dismiss it again."

After she'd hung up she dialled the operator again and asked for the charges.

On her way through the church she saw David Chandler up in the organ loft, and she opened the door and climbed the stairs. He had wooden machine parts laid out on the floor, and he was down on both knees measuring them and making drawings.

"Mrs. Giroux," he said and stood up. "I heard from Morris. Father William had to tell him because of the arrest situation."

"I see. So it's out."

"Well, yes. Do let me know if there's any way I can help. I mean, you not being able to get about. It must be some kind of mistake."

"It's not a mistake, Mr. Chandler. It's a long story and I thought it was over."

She stood looking down at the wooden parts on the floor. Drive shafts, universal joints, pedal links. There were two she did not recognize, and she used them to change the topic.

"What are those, Mr. Chandler?"

"The bellows levers. Pump levers, I should say. I'm thinking we could make them with a brass sleeve right there in the pivot where this one's cracked. There's friction, and any grease or graphite just gets squeezed out. I've done it before, using soft brass bearings instead of lubrication. When they fail you can replace just the sleeves. By the way, Mrs. Giroux, I have the first pair of shoes ready for you to try on. I can come by this afternoon, like you said. Would four o'clock be convenient?"

"Yes, it would." She waved a hand at the machine parts on the floor. "When I was young we made some of those for an organ company in Bordeaux. We used winter oak cut during the last few days of the new moon of January. There were a few people in our town who still knew about that sort of thing, and they had stories of wooden eavestroughs lasting two generations, and wooden shingles holding up longer than clay tiles. In the end we lost the contract to a Belgian company. They had cheaper wood from the Congo. A black, very hard wood. *Bois de fer*, we called it."

"I think in English it's also called ironwood, Mrs. Giroux. There's a version of it in North America. I don't know if it's black, but from what I hear it's hard enough on tools. And I've read about winter wood cut by the moon."

"Yes," she said. She hesitated a moment and then nodded at him and said she did not want to keep him. She walked away down the stairs, holding on to the wooden rail.

~

Back in Montmagny after the interminable return journey, she and Juliette took turns at Mother's bedside. Mother had become pale and thin, and she lay with her eyes closed much of the time. She had difficulty breathing; at times her breath stopped altogether and then restarted with a convulsive effort.

"A grave illness," Dr. Menasse said to Hélène after one of his visits. "I am quite certain now what it is."

"You are? What, doctor?"

"It's a form of cancer, Madame. In the lungs, mostly. But perhaps also the liver and the spleen."

He said he'd sent slides of blood and saliva to a laboratory and had viewed some slides himself under a microscope.

"Perhaps the fumes in the factory," he said. "The shellac and the glue. We know that solvents can change the chemistry of blood, which would then affect vital organs. And all that wood dust, fine cellulose clogging the lungs."

He looked down into the black crown of his hat and said, "The hospital might be a better place for her now, Madame."

And so Mother was moved to the Misericordia, and Hélène rode there twice a day on her bicycle. Juliette would take a taxi and spend hours at Mother's bedside and help the nurses look after her.

Hélène ordered cartons of surgical masks and made it a rule that they be worn by everyone on the factory floor. Claire had to put one on when she walked through the door, and Hélène wore one as well. When she saw men not wearing a mask, she called them into her mother's office one by one and sat them down and spoke to them. In the finishing room she had a second exhaust fan put into the exterior wall and more filtered air intakes in the wall opposite.

Mother, who had always been so relentlessly clear-minded and strong-willed, who had been able to wrestle the cast-iron harp for a baby grand onto a dolly and drag it across the floor to the place of assembly, could now hardly lift a cup to her lips.

Hélène rinsed her mother's face and did her hair and put lipstick on her lips, and her mother was so thankful for each small kindness it made Hélène want to weep.

They were working long hours to fill the orders coming in now from all over, she told Mother. Business was good, and since there was a bit of money now she was speaking to an engineering firm about electrifying the system. Apparently it could be done by widening the millrace at the top and narrowing it at the end, and then by replacing the old wooden water wheel with some kind of in-stream system with several rows of blades for much more power. A dynamo would then be connected for stronger electricity than was available on the house current. This would speed up all the wood preparation, and it would eliminate the dangerous and antiquated transmission belts on the floor.

Mother listened. She closed her eyes and said, "Good, Hélène. You are strong and courageous, and your heart is set to the truth. You'll do well. I know it absolutely."

"Thank you, Maman. Juliette has offered to move into the house. She thinks she can help me better that way. Should I accept?"

"No. Juliette likes her independence, and if she moves out of that little apartment she'll never get it back. Thank her, but say no."

"All right. I will. She still comes every day, and when I'm late she and Claire eat dinner together and then Juliette reads to her and puts her to bed. I offered to hire someone to help with Claire but Juliette won't hear of it."

"Of course not. Have a stranger in the house? Pay her a little more. Don't ask, just put more in the envelope. Refuse to discuss it."

There were sixteen beds in the cancer room. Visitors came and left, and doctors and nurses made their rounds in felt-soled hospital clogs. When a patient was close to death the nurses put screens around the bed, but the screens could not keep out the sounds. In a patient's last hours Father Dubert appeared and he whispered in Latin behind the screens, and they could hear the clinking of the glass stopper and those nearby could smell the scent of holy oil. Then the bed was rolled out the door and away to the right, down the hallway to where there was a swinging door with a creaking hinge whose sound everyone in the cancer room came to know very well. Next day the bed came back empty with fresh sheets and a clean name slate on it.

Once in a while Claire came along to visit Mother, but whenever she did she sat terrified and silent in the chair, and on the way home in the taxi she cried, and all the next day she hardly spoke.

Patients with money died more easily because they could pay for morphine. Mother could; Molnar pianos had perhaps killed her, but if so they were now also providing the means to help her be calm and breathe.

They were paying for a kinder death, *une mort plus douce*, Dr. Menasse said.

―――

On one of her last days, Mother gave her the most valuable gift she'd ever given her. It was after lunch on a cloudy day, with the light dim and gentle in the room. The food tray had been taken away, and Mother was sitting up against the pillow with her eyes closed. Hélène thought she was sleeping, but suddenly without opening her eyes Mother said softly, "I know you're there. I always know it. Give Claire my love. Kiss her for me and tell her not to come any more. But there is something I want to say to you, Hélène. I remembered it last night . . . I know you'll do your best with the business, but also never neglect your music. Businesses can disappear through no fault of our own, but your music is all yours. Look after it, and it will see you through." Her mother opened her eyes and looked at Hélène. "Have I told you that before?"

"No, you haven't, Maman. Not in that way." She reached and held her mother's hand on the blanket.

"Music did see *me* through, Hélène. Especially after your father died. In different ways, because I was never as good as you. But even so, our pianos gave me a wonderful purpose all my life. Your father and you and our fine pianos."

"Yes, Maman."

"I know your father was not home very much, but I also know that he was unhappy about that. He would have loved to spend more time with you. The Colonial Office pays them well, but it also works them like slaves . . . Things weren't always easy between your father and me. Perhaps you know that, or perhaps you don't. It doesn't matter. It's much more important that you know I loved your father. I came to love him very much . . . For a while after he died it was very hard. I felt so lost, sweetheart, but eventually I learned things about myself that I would never have learned otherwise. Even so, nothing was ever the same. Am I repeating myself? Have I said that before?"

"No, you haven't, Maman. And if you have, it doesn't matter. I like to hear you talk about Papa."

She was weeping by then. She wanted to wipe her eyes, but she would not let go of her mother's hand for fear of losing her.

Two days later the screens were put around the bed, and when Father Dubert arrived in his vestments and with the holy oil, her mother's face relaxed in the most beautiful way.

Pierre could not come in time for the funeral, but to her surprise Nathan was there. And so on a November afternoon they all stood at the graveside while Father Dubert waved his censer and prayed in Latin. When he said *Amen*, they all replied *Amen* and crossed themselves, and then she and Claire took turns with the silver cup, and they scooped up earth and let it fall on Mother's coffin. She crouched beside Claire and held her close. Nathan stood not far away with his head bowed and his hat in his hands. She avoided looking at him, but she was always aware of him; in her state of grief he was a distraction, and she wished he hadn't come.

"Help me fend him off," she whispered to Juliette, and from behind her black veil Juliette said, "Don't worry about him."

He had a car waiting and he offered them a ride, but she thanked him and said they'd rather walk, it was not far. Juliette motioned him aside, and after a few paces when Hélène looked back she saw them standing on the grass by the walkway, Nathan tall in a trench coat with a black mourning band on the sleeve and Juliette frail but still so very straight in a long black coat and black hat with the veil folded up now, and Juliette's hand was halfway up and moving sideways in some firm gesture of refusal.

"He invited us for dinner," Juliette said later, "but I explained that none of us is up to socializing. Still, he will be calling in the morning to say his adieus. That is something we cannot deny him."

In the morning she and Nathan took coffee in the library. Juliette served them on the good sterling tray and then hovered in the background like a chaperone. Nathan sat in his chair, confident and with the familiar spark in his eyes.

He was doing well, he said when she asked him. He was working for the Egypt Antiquities Service, learning a great deal about that new field. He talked about the Valley of the Kings and the tombs, all the amazing treasures being unearthed there.

He said, "It's giving me ideas for a lucrative business of my own, Helen. In museum pieces."

"Not pianos any more?"

He shook his head.

"And how did you know about Mother?"

"Oh. I just heard, I forget from whom. Someone in Amsterdam, I think. Molnar is becoming quite a name."

When he stood up to leave, he said, "If there's ever anything I can do to help – anything. For old times' sake, and because I always thought highly of your mother."

He waited. "Helen? I want you to know that I am very happy for you. Your marriage, your lovely daughter. You in charge at Molnar now. Congratulations. I am glad things turned out well for you. They did for me too."

"Yes, it sounds like it. I'm glad, Nathan."

She walked with him downstairs and smiled and shook his hand at the door. He leaned and kissed her cheek.

"An interesting man," said Juliette afterward. "More so than most. We have to admit that. But an adventurer, to hear him speak. Men like that do not make good husbands, Hélène. Strong, steady men do. Like your Pierre. You made the right choice."

~

The pair of shoes that David Chandler brought in the early evening felt better than any she'd ever had on her feet. She sat on the chair by the coal fire and slipped them on and off, and on again. She stood up and walked to the window and back.

"Is there good support where you need it, Mrs. Giroux?"

"Yes. It seems very good, Mr. Chandler. Loose on top, of course, without laces, but firm where it matters."

"If you step this way, we'll pinch it where the laces will be. Make it snug around the ankles. The foot changes shape as we put weight on it. And it needs to be able to move forward a bit, maybe an eighth of an inch."

"It feels very good."

"Did you want hooks and eyelets, or just eyelets?"

"Perhaps just eyelets. That seems to be the fashion now."

"It is. Very well then."

"Shall we have our tea now, Mr. Chandler?"

"I would like that, Mrs. Giroux."

She made tea, and when she brought the tray from the kitchen he was standing by the window looking out. There were two windows in the living room, and this one faced southwest onto the ocean. The sky was deep red along the horizon and nearly purple above.

"Beautiful," he said. "I imagine on a clear day you can see Maine, and some nights you might even see lights refracting up from below the earth's curvature. That would be Eastport then, or Cutler. Grand Manan would be more that way. You wouldn't see it for the trees."

He took a few sips of tea and carried cup and saucer to the coffee table. They sat on the sofa and the chair in the light from the floor lamp.

"You notice I'm not asking any questions, Mrs. Giroux. I'm sure whatever it is, it'll all get cleared up, but in the meantime, like I said, I'd be glad to lend a hand. Just send someone to let me know."

"Thank you, Mr. Chandler."

For a moment all was quiet except for some seagulls in the distance.

"I'm from New York City myself," he said then. "My parents used to come here with us for the summers so my sister and I could get the air, as they used to say. I always liked it, and when they died I moved here. My sister moved to California. We still write."

"And you learned the business here?"

"The leatherwork, yes. In New York I studied engineering and pattern making, and then here I learned the leatherwork. It's good to have a second arrow to one's quiver. And it's interesting. I've been lucky in many ways in my life, Mrs. Giroux. Not in all. I was married for sixteen years, and then my wife died with the Spanish flu. Early on in the epidemic. Quite a few people did, in these parts."

"I'm sorry to hear that, Mr. Chandler. I was in London at the time, and we had it there too. I knew some who died from it. My daughter and I were lucky."

"Your daughter," he said and smiled. "Tell me about her."

She rose from the chair and found her purse and took out the small leather folder with Claire's photograph and handed it to him. "This was taken five or six years ago in Montreal. In the backyard of the house where we lived for many years. I too have been lucky in many ways, Mr. Chandler, but not in all. In one important event I was not lucky. But at least my situation now does give me time to think. That is the silver lining. I don't need to look over my shoulder all the time any more, and I can slow down and prepare myself for what is coming."

"Yes," he said. "I think I know what you mean." He put the photo down on the table and waited a moment, and when she offered no more he said, "About the shoes now – the right one would be the more critical, and it's fine, you say?"

"It's more than fine. It's very good. Thank you, Mr. Chandler. By the way, did you mean that, that you'd be prepared to lend a hand?"

"Yes, I do. I certainly do."

"Good. Because there is something. We were speaking of Claire just now – well, you'll be meeting her soon because she's coming to visit, and I was wondering, Mr. Chandler: Can you drive a car?"

Ten

PIERRE HAD A TELEPHONE installed at the Tonkin Hill house, and over a relay of Colonial Office exchanges they would talk at prearranged times. The Vietminh attacks had flared up again, and he had been put in charge of a company of Foreign Legionnaires to patrol the countryside and plantations. He was losing men to explosives buried in dirt roads, he said. Dynamite, triggered by someone stepping on a crude switch. Grenades tripped by wires on bush paths. His men were also falling into hidden pits spiked with sharpened bamboo sticks smeared with excrement. But the enemy was never seen. They moved by night; they blended in with the local population.

She asked if he should be telling her these things on the telephone, and he said it did not matter. Everybody knew. He sounded tired.

"They hate us," he said. "That is a well-known fact too.

The upper classes still love us and they welcome our money and the jobs, but not these rebels."

"And you?" she said. "Your own safety? I worry about you. We miss you."

"Oh, I'm fine, sweetheart. I have developed a sixth sense about the dangers here."

In the newspapers, she read that Indochina was not the only place where colonial trouble was stirring; hatred of the foreign exploiter, of the self-appointed, pale-faced overlord, was rising like the tide everywhere: in India and in Africa and many other places; against the British and the French and the Germans; against the Belgians and the Portuguese; and, in their own corners of the Far East, against the Dutch. In Eastern Europe against the Austrians.

In February 1914, Pierre was recalled and permitted a short leave before being reassigned. He stepped off the train, thin and yellow-eyed with tropical fevers, and she and Claire took him home in a horse-drawn carriage and put him straight to bed. Dr. Menasse examined his blood and in it found microscopic creatures, self-propelling forms of life, he said, that he did not recognize. He sent a report to the Ministry of Health in Paris, and their colonial office sent vials of a drug to be injected into Pierre's veins.

At first he got worse, then he got better. By then the Austrian archduke and his wife had been shot dead and all the Balkans were in turmoil. The papers were full of speculation and fearful predictions. Juliette said that war was coming, anyone could feel that. She said she was old enough to remember 1870. Every generation had its own war, but perhaps hers had two. Perhaps not, said Hélène. Perhaps the politicians had learned from the last one. But Juliette only shook her head and turned away.

In those days Hélène was torn in several directions at once: having Pierre in the house was new and mostly wonderful, but she also had a factory to run and orders for pianos to fill. Her workers depended on her.

The electrification of the plant had been undertaken, but because a Molnar piano was in every single stage still made by hand, the increase in production efficiency was less than she'd hoped. Monsieur Bendix Raoul had predicted as much, when she'd first consulted him; now, rather than remind her of that, he said that with the transmission belts gone the factory was much safer, and the power was good and constant whether the water in the river ran high or low.

Less than a month later, war did break out.

It happened on a day when she was in the cork room voicing a piano for a St. Petersburg dealer, struggling with the subtlety of a triple string, closing her eyes and cocking her head to the sounds with absolute concentration, striking the key again and again, and then making the tiniest shifts of the pins – tiny, tiny nudges, hardly any movement at all. This, while all over the country and all over Europe newspaper presses fell silent and a new headline was inserted or a special edition set. That evening she read it in *Le Figaro*.

Pierre received his orders, and he was pleased about them. He tried not to show it, but she could tell. Honourable action for a soldier at home, he said to her. A known enemy who would fight in the open, not by night and with booby traps. But no serious threat for the French army, he assured her. Such discipline and excellent training and leadership. It would be over soon. Perhaps not by Christmas as the newspapers were saying, but certainly by spring.

There was time for a short holiday before he had to report for duty, and they travelled by train to the Belgian town of Oostende and stayed at a resort hotel. They walked the beach at low tide and they swung Claire between them and watched her do cartwheels. She was so much in love with her little family, the three of them so fortunate, with a fine protective light around them. They rented a beach boat on wheels, and they skimmed along with the wind filling the sail and wet sand arching high in their wake. At night in the hotel she and Pierre had a room to themselves, and they made love to sweet exhaustion. They slept in each other's arms as they had done in the house on Tonkin Hill, except that in Oostende in the morning a maid knocked and brought them breakfast in bed. Soon after that Claire would come bouncing in from the adjoining room, wide awake and impatient for the new day's adventure.

On August 30 of that year, the military sent Pierre to take command of a company in the east, and just five weeks later he was dead. A hero, his colonel's letter said; one who'd given his life for France during a dawn attack on enemy lines. They sent his medals and his wallet, and a wedding ring that was not his. In the wallet, she found among other bits of paper a small print of the picture that the magazine had taken of her, and another picture of Claire looking scrubbed and uncommonly serene in her sailor suit, also taken by the magazine photographer.

The day after the letter, she and Claire took out the black clothes they'd bought for her mother's funeral. Claire had started school that year; she'd outgrown the dress and Hélène bought a new one.

Juliette came along as they walked to her mother's grave, and then they stood there for a while because they needed to stand at a grave that day.

It was another golden October day, much like the one ten years ago when she'd sat with Pierre eating ice cream and watching his face and promising herself that this would never change. Shiny chestnuts lay on the ground again, and from somewhere beyond the cemetery wall came the sounds of boys shouting and the thump of a ball. Eventually they turned and walked away along the gravel path.

"We are not alone, sweetheart," she said thickly to Claire. "We are still a family." And Claire looked up to search her face behind the veil and held her hand more tightly.

Eleven

THERE HAD BEEN A TIME when she disliked having
to play the piano, playing for prospective buyers, always
having to dress up as she had for the man from Boston,
her hair always up because her mother insisted that there
was a sweet vulnerability to a young woman's neck.

"They're not buying *me*, Maman," she'd objected at first.
And her mother had said, "No, they're not, sweetheart. But
something lovely attaches to the piano, and they like that.
They'll remember it. A moment of our exceptional culture,
in their all-too-familiar English or American drawing-rooms
back home. That is what they're buying, Hélène: memories
and dreams, and our wonderful pianos."

But if she'd hated playing the piano then, it was saving
her life now, had been doing so for years.

She was at the keyboard, working from memory on
"Morning Has Broken," when she saw Father William
entering by the side door. He looked at her across the
sanctuary and then came her way. She stopped playing.

"It's a new hymn," she said. "Do you know it?"

"I don't think so."

"The words are by an Englishwoman called Eleanor Farjeon, and they are set to a Gaelic tune. It's lovely. Listen."

She played and sang it for him softly:

Morning has broken like the first morning;
Blackbird has spoken like the first bird;
Praise for the singing, praise for the morning;
Praise for them springing fresh from the Word . . .

"Yes, lovely," he said. "Lovely."

"I'd like to find the sheet music so I can work on it with the choir."

"We can probably get it in the city. There's a good music store on Barrington Street. I'll telephone them."

He looked up and around. There were perhaps a dozen people sitting in pews in the dim light near the door.

"You have an audience."

"Yes. They started coming the day after I put up the notice."

"I'm glad to see you are able to think about music. How are you coming along with the choir?"

"Quite well. We've met six or seven times now. The new situation is not helping, but I've spoken to them and asked them to put all that aside until the court case, and most are quite good about it. One or two are resisting me, but I can deal with it." She looked at her watch. "I could stop now. There is something I want to talk to you about. Do you have a minute?"

"Yes, of course. Before I forget, the sergeant said he couldn't allow an improperly registered car to be parked in a public place. He brought a form for you to fill out, and he'll issue a temporary permit and registration at the church address."

"Good. Please tell him I thank him for that. And by the way, David Chandler will be asking you for the car keys. He'll be running an errand for me."

In the vestry he closed the door after her, and then they sat facing each other across the table corner.

"You understand that you do not have to tell me anything, Mrs. Giroux. I've thought about it, and under the circumstances it might be better if you didn't say things that could create a conflict. For either of us. Unless it's under the seal of confession, and even that might not be advisable."

She shook her head. "There'll be no conflict. And I have nothing to confess. But I do want you to know what that policeman was talking about. You were right. I should have told you when we first spoke, but I was hoping to begin anew here, and I felt it might spoil my chances. You've been very kind to me, and you continue to be, and so I want to tell you about that photo in his file."

"If you wish."

"Father William, do you know where museums get most of their exhibits from? I don't think anyone does, so I'll tell you. Some are donated, some are on loan, but most are bought for lots of money. But bought from whom? Who would have the right to sell these things? National treasures, many of them. Entire altars carted away from temples in Indochina and erected in museums in London and Paris. Burial gifts from Egypt, scrolls, tablets. Mummies and bones. *Bones.* You get the idea. And now that colonialism is coming to an end, there is an enormous rush for artifacts from foreign lands. The money involved, the competition and even thievery, you cannot imagine . . .

"A few years ago I was travelling the colonial world with the man the sergeant mentioned. Nathan Homewood. He was in the business of finding and buying museum exhibits, and I was helping him. On one trip in northern Alberta, he died under terrible circumstances, and I was the only person on the scene."

He held up a hand to stop her. "I'll remind you that you don't have to tell me any of this."

"I know I don't *have* to, but I want to. It matters to me what you and a few others here think of me. So please listen . . .

"I know very well that by the time they found us, I was not myself any more. That photograph you saw in the sergeant's file was taken after they released me from the institution. I certainly remember *that* place, naked in a cage and cold water from a hose – to cure me of my madness, they said. It was in all the papers, at least out west, and in France. I was charged with the worst offence anyone could be charged with, and the trial went on for two weeks. Then the judge said there was not enough evidence to support the charge, and I was acquitted."

She watched him, his open face and young eyes trying to sort all this fairly and not to show shock or disapproval.

"William," she said. "Father William. Those are the facts. The charge was murder. I can say that now and admit it to you and to myself, and it is a relief. You can tell people. Mr. Chandler too, and Mildred. I don't mind; in fact, I'd like you to tell them. Before long it'll all be out anyway, and I'd prefer it if they heard it from you rather than through gossip and speculation. Tell them, so that the next time I see someone I won't have to say anything, but I'll know what it is they know because it came from you."

Twelve

LATER CLAIRE WOULD describe how she'd taken the Zeppelin to New York and the train from there to Portland and the ferry across the Gulf of Maine to Yarmouth. David Chandler had stood at the dockside, and because she was dressed for winter and the electric light was poor, he did not recognize her. But she was the only young woman travelling alone, dressed in a coat and hat with a tired face and searching eyes, and so he'd walked up to her and showed her the photo in the little folder and introduced himself.

He'd carried the suitcase to the Austin and put it in the trunk, and then he brought her north along the coastal road to Saint Homais. They talked, but not much. She'd explained that she was very tired. *Fifty-three hours since London, Mr. Chandler*, she'd said.

For stretches along the dark road it had snowed, and when the flakes came dense and near-horizontal at the head-lights, he'd shifted down into first gear and carried on.

———

While she waited for them she kept getting up from the chair and walking to the window. Several times she opened it and breathed in the cold, fresh air and leaned out to see past the church to the main street. It was empty and silent. No cars or horses, no people, no activity at all. Thick snowflakes like fog in the circles of light from the streetlamps.

She walked back into the kitchen, where she was keeping warm some seafood bisque of Mildred's in case Claire was hungry. She added a little water and stirred and put the lid back on and returned to the window. Around ten she lay down on the sofa to close her eyes for a moment, and she woke nearly an hour later to sounds in the street. From the window she saw the car and Claire talking through the half-open door and then closing it. Hélène hurried down the stairs to meet her.

"Claire, sweetheart. You must be tired. I'm so glad you're here. I'm keeping something warm for you to eat, if you want it."

Claire looked at the steep stairs going up. "Mom," she said, "right now I'm past being hungry, and I'm so tired I can't even talk properly. I just wanted to come in and hug you. Mr. Chandler is waiting in the car."

"Of course. I understand. I booked you a room at the hotel, like we said. But after tomorrow I want you to sleep here. Take the bed and I'll sleep on the sofa."

"Sure. Or the other way round. I'll see you in the morning. I'm glad I'm here too, Mom."

Hélène lay awake until past two in the morning, then she got up and heated some milk. She held the mug with both hands and stood once again at the window. She could not see the hotel, but it would be over that way, to the right. Darkness out there. Silence. More snow.

~

By the time Pierre was dead, all activity at the factory had already ceased. In the crating room pianos stood ready for shipment, but transport for anything other than war essentials was no longer available. Half the men in her workforce had been drafted, and she'd taken all the business money and her own out of the bank and paid them off generously. The others she tried to keep on, but in the end she paid them off too and gave them a bonus and sent them home. Monsieur Bendix Raoul received one full year's extra pay. On the day he came to say goodbye, she did not recognize him at first. He wore an old black suit and a white shirt, and he stood in the main hall with his hands hanging idle and a cardboard suitcase at his feet. He looked around and took his time, and he nodded slowly as though this were the way it was all meant to be. He turned to her and said, "Madame . . ." but then words failed him, and she went up to him and took his hand. Minutes later he was gone. The man-door to the hall stood open to a bright fall day, and all the factory was silent.

_____

For the rest of 1914 and 1915 the area was occupied by the French with artillery positions and supply and hospital services. Later that year came the British, and the war went on and on. In January of 1916 the Germans broke through and came very close; there was fierce fighting before they were driven back again. During that time the factory suffered serious damage when shells burst nearby and shattered one wall and parts of the roof. And always soldiers from one army or another took shelter or were being officially housed there. They made fires for light and heat in the scrap bins, and they used kiln wood and crating wood for fuel. When that ran out they broke up piano cabinet pieces ready for assembly.

She'd spoken to the first few officers about that, and they always promised to talk to the men, but if they did, it never made any difference. Often she could see smoke rising from the factory windows. She did not go down any more.

Fortunately the best and most expensive wood was stored in the loft of the barn, hidden under straw, and somehow that wood survived: rare winter oak and English walnut and precious Scandinavian clear spruce for sound-boards, and the remaining rolls of fruit-tree veneer from the orchard across the river.

The main house was occupied by a succession of officers who permitted her and Claire to stay in two rooms on the top floor. Juliette hardly ever came to the house any more: the squire's lodge was close to the church, and she had begun to cook for the priest and eat her meals at the manse.

In the salon at the main house there was a grand piano, and in return for their protection and for food from the field kitchen, Hélène played for the officers. Most often the food was some kind of one-pot meal, often horsemeat and root vegetables boiled together. Sometimes potato or beet pancakes or some kind of noodle dish. At first she'd been able to catch a trout or two on a line from the mill walk. But then soldiers killed all the fish with grenades and netted them, and that was the end of that.

The officers, whether they were French or British, were usually well-bred young men. They washed and even dressed for dinner and then pretended life was normal as they sat on the blue sofa or on a stuffed chair and listened to her playing the piano.

There was one young man, Captain Francis Huxtable from Kent, who wept when she played some late Brahms. She caught him wiping his eyes. Two days later he was dead, replaced already by another young captain, who was himself dead within the week. It was as though there were an endless supply of young men lining up for the slaughter and dropping dead only to make room for a new eager head to show itself above the corpses.

One day in the autumn of 1916, when the British were holding the ground, Nathan Homewood appeared. He came in a Morris field car, wearing a uniform. He said he'd learned only a month ago that Pierre had been killed early in the war; if he'd known, he would have come sooner.

He told her he'd been too old to be drafted in the first round for active service, but because of his experience he'd been enlisted as a logistics officer in the Canadian transport corps.

"How can I help?" he said. "Please allow me, Helen. What can I do?"

He unpacked bread and cheese and tinned food and two bottles of wine and even chocolate. They fetched Juliette from the squire's lodge and then they had a feast by candle-light because most of the electricity no longer worked. They sat around the bed in the upstairs room, eating from the bedcover like at a picnic.

She was glad to see him and feel his energy and the ray of hope he brought. That night she gave up her room for him, and as she said good night he gave her a questioning look but she pretended not to notice and closed the door.

In the morning he inspected the factory, and when he came back upstairs he shook his head. "My God," he said. "I can see why you don't want to go down any more. It would break your heart. From what I've seen there is no longer any reason for you to wait out the war here. There's nothing left to guard, and England or Canada would be much safer for you now. Do you have any money?"

"Not much any more."

"I see. You'd need money, Helen. Is there anything you can sell?"

"Sell? Where?"

"Not here, obviously. In England, or in America. I'm there every other month."

"Well, I still have my mother's placement sketches for the different models. Sketches in great detail, like an engineer's drawings. You saw how exacting she was. They are of no use to me now, but they might be worth something to another piano company. And there's the wood."

"What wood?"

That night she took him to the barn and showed him where the ladder was hidden and how to reach the upper level. She held the flashlight while he scooped away straw and ran his hand over the exquisite wood.

"Fantastic," he said. "How much of it is there?"

"A lot. A hundred thousand francs of it. Maybe more. What's that in dollars? Ten, twenty thousand? It's pure gold to an instrument maker. No knots, no cracks, nothing warped. If we could sell it, the money would keep Claire and me safe for years. Here in this barn all it would take is one fool to make a fire like they did in the factory."

"Exactly. I think I know where there might be a market. How much is there in volume? Or how much weight?"

She did not know. They looked down the hatch to make sure that no one had followed them and then he spent another ten minutes measuring the stacks by pacing them off and using an improvised yardstick for height and width.

"There's maybe as much as eight or nine hundred cubic feet," he said then. "It's amazing. We'll need more than one truck."

He climbed down first and held the ladder for her.

They could make some sort of deal, she said. Perhaps one-third for him, would that be fair? Or even one-half, if he managed to get a good price.

"We'll see. Helen . . ." He stopped and stood looking at her. He seemed shy suddenly, and he opened his mouth to continue but then he turned away. The next day he left again.

In January 1917 she played for an army surgeon from Metz, a major in his late thirties. He wanted to practise a four-handed Czerny with her, and he was good, with a promising touch on the keys. She taught him to lengthen his hand and to slow down, and when practising to concentrate on each single note, since each note was the only one that mattered.

When he was not playing he sat on the blue sofa smoking Balkan Sobranje cigarettes and sipping Calvados. She watched him lighting his cigarettes at the top of the lamp funnel, and as he did so the flame from below made his face hollow-cheeked and hollow-eyed, a death mask already. He lasted not quite five weeks and died from blood poisoning after a patient struggled during an amputation and some instrument slipped and tore his hand.

All the time under the French, the factory served as a field hospital. It overflowed quickly and then the yard too filled with stretchers. When the ground was frozen, the dead were carted away a distance but not quite out of sight from her bedroom window. They were stacked like cord-wood under the willows, row after row in torn, bloody uniforms or stained white shifts that stirred in the breeze. Crows came in vast flocks, a glistening, swarming carpet of them, and they shrieked and hacked at the corpses. At night dogs came and snarled and fought over the remains.

In the spring of 1917 the ground thawed and so did the dead by the willows. A tank with a trench blade ripped up the earth, and then a dozen soldiers dragged the bodies one by one to the hole and laid them down. Lime was poured on them and it drifted in white clouds, and then the tank pushed the earth back over the dead. A French chaplain in uniform with a purple stole around his neck waited upwind from it all, and when it was done he made the sign of the cross in the air.

In the summer the Canadians rotated through the sector, and during that time she housed a young battery commander from Montreal, a blond, wavy-haired captain named Xavier Boucher. He was the first of the officers she found attractive as a man. What she also liked about him was the effect he had on Claire. Claire was nine, and the years since her father's death had changed her from a spunky tomboy turning cartwheels into a sad child who'd forgotten how to smile or play. But Xavier had a youthful sense of humour, and despite the horrors he could make her and Claire laugh. He played ball with Claire in the salon because they could not go down into the yard, and in the light from the oil lamp against the wall he showed her how to make shadow animals with her hands: a rabbit, a cow, a goat, a chicken; a farmyard full of animals, and a barking dog to guard them.

For him too, Hélène played in the evening. One night she played the "Moonlight Sonata" and "Für Elise," and later when Claire was long in bed in the upstairs room she allowed him the first intimacies. The next night she let him make love to her because she wanted the comfort and sweetness as much as he.

They lay in the dark on her mother's blue sofa and distant explosions painted the window cross onto the ceiling. When he was asleep in that shifting light, she kept watch over him, and she could see his face, tired and surely a bit younger than she but already in command of a company of men who would look to him for courage and leadership in the pointless horrors of battle.

Less than four weeks later he told them that his unit was being broken up and repositioned. He did not know where to. He said so over dinner and, when she heard that, Claire put down her fork and looked at him round-eyed.

In the early morning he left and the door closed behind him. His batman came and packed his bag. Later they could hear commands and she and Claire watched from a window, the men forming ranks, engines pulling field pieces, and they could see him on a chestnut horse at the point of a column, far away, perhaps a hundred and fifty yards in the field. He raised an arm and put his horse forward.

That same day some other Canadian unit dug a field-gun position a hundred yards behind the house, and sometimes in the nights to come, she and Claire would stand at the window and watch as shells roared overhead and then set the world on fire.

Enemy shells were landing ever closer, and the interlocked fronts sawed back and forth – seven kilometres from the factory, ten, twenty, then ten again. Flares exploded into white light in mid-air and sank back to earth on small silken parachutes. They drifted before the wind like brilliant stars, and some would come as far as the millpond and drown with quick puffs of smoke.

A month later Nathan returned with three covered Bedford trucks, and within hours the wood was brought down from the barn loft and loaded onto the truck beds.

He told her he now had excellent contacts in Britain and Canada, and through them he'd been able to arrange transport to Canada for the wood.

"For free, Helen. It'll be part of the ballast in an empty troop ship going back. Bricks and your wood. It's going to a piano and organ factory in Ontario. The ship will dock in Halifax and the wood continues by rail. And there's more, Helen. I can get you and Claire to England. We'll have to leave in the morning."

"*Tomorrow* morning?"

"Yes."

She said she'd think about it.

"Think about it? You're beginning to sound like your mother. What is there to think about? I am offering to save your lives. Sooner or later this stretch will be the front itself, and I have seen what happens to cities in the front line. They become rubble. Caves and corpses and rats."

"How much will they give us for the wood, Nathan? I'll pay you a commission, like I said."

"Never mind that. I'm glad I can help." He looked at her and grinned and offered his hand. "Friends, Helen. Last time I still had hopes, I don't know why, but I've given up. You can go on loving your dead Pierre, and you and I, we'll just be friends from now on. All right?"

She shook his hand happily. "How much money will they be paying us, Nathan?"

"A few thousand Canadian dollars. They need to see it, and then they'll mention an exact amount."

"How much in francs, more or less?"

"That's hard to say, because who knows what the franc is worth now. They want to see the charts as well. Don't forget them."

"All right. And listen, Nathan. I wonder if you could make some inquiries for us. A little while ago we had a French-Canadian captain billeted here. His unit was moved, but if possible we'd like to keep in touch with him."

"Keep in touch? What for?"

"For Claire's sake. He was very nice to her."

"A captain? What was his name?"

"Xavier Boucher. He was a battery commander."

"All right. I'll see what I can do."

That same evening one of the trucks took them past army tents to the squire's lodge. Outside one tent they saw Nathan with some Canadian soldiers, playing cards. He looked up and waved.

At the lodge they sat with Juliette in her apartment: Juliette on the bed, Hélène on the only chair, and Claire on the floor. One of the two windows was broken, and the glass had been replaced with cardboard. For furniture there was only the bed and the chair and a rug from Juliette's mother, a small desk with two candlesticks, a vanity with an untrue mirror, an armoire, and a few pictures on the wall.

Juliette saw her looking around, and she smiled and said, "The bare essentials, Hélène. It's interesting how little one really needs and how everything else can come to feel like a burden."

"Juliette," she said. "Nathan has found a way to sell our wood for us. And he wants us to leave with him, tomorrow morning. I'm still undecided. The trucks would drive to the coast, and a ship would take us to England. You could come with us."

Juliette sat with her thin shoulders back and her hands in her lap. Her nails were manicured, and Hélène could see that she'd rinsed her hair in the purple dye for which the chemist had been making the effervescent powder for years and selling it in sachets for a centime.

She smiled at Hélène and shook her head. "No, dear. Thank you, but no. You are still young, and our Claire here is just starting out. If only for her sake, the two of you should leave, and if Nathan is offering you a chance to escape and turn the wood into money, you must take it."

"And you?"

"I'll stay, of course. At my age I'd much rather be here than be a refugee in some English city where I'll never belong. I can see the end of it, Hélène. It was interesting at times but long enough, really, and this is how it should be. I think you know what I mean."

"Nathan says the front is coming closer. Their shells may soon be reaching the city."

"Perhaps."

They sat a while longer. Light flickered through summer trees out the window. Distant explosions.

"But what are you going to do?"

"Do? I'll continue to cook for the Father. Farmers still bring him food. He's a decent man who may even believe what he preaches, but he doesn't expect me to. So we get along fine. And I'm writing again. At the moment I am writing a poem about light, how it changes and how all things look different then. It's one of my better insights and I keep coming back to it. It won't go anywhere but that's all right. I'll be fine, Hélène. I'm not worried about a single thing."

They sat in silence while the finality of all this sank in.

After some time Juliette said kindly, "You should go, Hélène. Before it gets dark. Claire, sweetheart, take your mother home. You need to pack."

That night a shell struck the barn and it burned for hours, with timbers and walls collapsing and flames and sparks dancing high. She and Claire sat on the side of the bed they'd been sharing again, looking out at the inferno. Claire, who'd been so good and courageous most of the time, wept and said it was all so very terrible and would it never end.

"It will end one day, sweetheart," she said, and held her close. "It will. It most definitely will. I promise you that."

In the morning they were on the second of the three trucks leaving the factory yard. Nathan was at the wheel and Claire sat between them. He was whistling softly, not with any real sound, just his breath curving tunelessly over his lips.

At some point when Hélène could not stand it any longer she snapped at him and asked him what there was to whistle about. He stopped.

"But you and Claire are safe now," he said. "The war is over for you. Isn't that something to be happy about?"

At Boulogne-sur-Mer they lined up for food at a Canadian field kitchen, and they sat on benches made from ammunition crates in a tent by the harbour wall. They ate fish cakes and rice from mess kits with folding spoons among hundreds of soldiers coming and going. Troop carriers lay at anchor and landing craft went back and forth.

Back at the trucks she handed Nathan her mother's drawings for the various piano models. He unrolled one and looked at it and shook his head.

"In such detail," he said.

Not far away engines started up and whistles blew and soldiers were forming a line.

"Nathan," she shouted over the noise. "This wood is top instrument grade. It's exceptionally valuable. And the wood and these sketches are all Claire and I have. Please tell me again what's going to happen."

"It goes as ballast in an empty ship to Halifax and from there by train to Ontario. They'll examine it and give us a fair price. The same with the drawings."

"I see. Nathan, I hope you won't misinterpret this, but do you think I could have a written record of this deal? I appreciate your offer to do it for free, but I'd like to give you a quarter of the money anyway. Please accept it, it's better that way. I'm going to write up the details of the transaction, and I'd like you to sign it."

"I can't do that, because of the War Materials Act. Why not just trust me?"

"I do trust you. God forbid, but what if something should happen to you?"

"You are not listening. With a piece of paper like that I'd be incriminating myself, and you. Shipping private cargo for sale. Your wood goes as unlisted ballast, so just be glad and trust the situation. Okay?"

"Not really. I have nothing to show for this deal. Couldn't the ship's captain give me a receipt?"

"The ship's captain. Of course not. Be sensible, Helen. And speaking of being sensible: I asked around but I couldn't find out anything about your captain and the French-Canadian unit."

"Nothing at all? No one knew anything?"

"No. Or if they did, they wouldn't say. It's war, Helen. And now Claire and you better get your bags out of the truck. We'll be boarding soon."

Thirteen

IN THE MORNING FRESH snow covered the street and all the roofs. Smoke rose from chimneys everywhere. It rose and blew sideways from the tin stack on the roof of what she knew by now was David Chandler's leather workshop.

At nine o'clock, Claire arrived with breakfast for two on a tray. She kicked off her boots and took off her coat and then they sat in the kitchen, drinking coffee and eating soft-boiled eggs and toast with strawberry jam.

Claire said, "I wrote the exam, and now I have maybe as much as three weeks' leave. But there's a paid intern position I applied for, and if I need to write some sort of follow-up paper, they'll telephone me. In that case I'd have to go back. By the way, I paid for the tickets from the special account like you said, and I took out another one hundred dollars and brought it for other expenses. Is that all right?"

"Of course it is."

"Is there an attorney in this town?"

"I don't know. I haven't asked anyone yet."

"I'll make some calls."

"The church office is ice-cold, so maybe do it from the telephone exchange. It's just past the Dominion Bank, and then you could stop in there and cash a cheque I'll give you so I can pay my bills here. They're all being very helpful. The priest is giving me this apartment in exchange for providing the church music. I'm just living on savings now, but I'll find a way to earn money again."

"I'm sure you will. Now tell me again what the policeman said."

"Just that there was new evidence and the case was being reopened. That's all."

"Can they do that, once it's dismissed?"

"Apparently so. A lawyer will know all that."

Claire left, and just an hour later she was back. She put a bank envelope on the kitchen table, took off her coat and then looked at her notes.

"One attorney I spoke to in Annapolis Royal said he remembered the case and it interested him. He said it was basically an *autrefois acquit*. A double jeopardy. He said there are very few exceptions that permit a retrial for murder. Wrong in law is one, and fresh evidence is another."

"Has he defended a case like this before?"

"I asked him that, and he said no. He said they're rare because of the strict exceptions. But procedurally they are no different from any other murder case."

"All right. Can he find out what the new evidence is?"

"Once he's taken on the case, he'll be in a position as your attorney to act on your behalf. He thinks the trial will be fairly soon. In a few weeks, maybe even before Christmas, with the circuit court that's booked to come through."

Later she was at the piano in the church for her regular afternoon practice session. She played Gabriel Fauré, and people whose faces she knew by now sat in pews listening, and more came in and took seats. The girl from the foundry office came, and so did David Chandler. He was carrying a brown paper bag and he settled into a pew and held the bag on his knees. She played on. It was exceptionally still in the church and the piano in its new place sounded wonderful. It also gave her a better view of the front of the church past the open lid, and to her right a wider view of the congregation.

Near the end of the piece, Claire came in and sat down next to David Chandler.

She played "In the Bleak Midwinter," and there was not one cough or shuffle to be heard in the church. Once she'd established the melody she started from the beginning and, guided by the fine lyrics, expanded it into a circular ballad of her own spontaneous creation.

> *In the bleak midwinter, frosty wind made moan,*
> *Earth stood hard as iron, water like a stone.*
> *Snow had fallen, snow on snow, snow on snow,*
> *In the bleak midwinter, long ago . . .*

~

From the moment they were on that Bedford truck leaving the factory yard, she and Claire were homeless. Refugees. Émigrés was the kinder notion, because it suggested an act of choice. They travelled to Portsmouth on a British ship taking back wounded and to return with more soldiers for the slaughter. Most of the way they kept to the deck because of the horror everywhere below. When the Isle of Wight came into clear view, she was at the railing next to Claire.

In Portsmouth the harbour was filled with soldiers in brown uniforms and shallow tin hats. They formed restless groups, grinning and joshing each other like excited boys off on a school trip, but then all movement stopped and they stared as the wounded were carried off and men with firehoses flushed decks and holds. Pumps came on and water foaming with blood and vomit gushed from the sides of the ship into the harbour.

———

In London they lived in a rented flat in East Kensington, with scarred furniture and bare floors until she was able to buy a few rugs with the money she earned teaching piano at the conservatory. Claire went to school and made friends in a class with other children from France and Belgium. She'd picked up some English from Nathan and the officers back in France, and that helped. Some days she brought one of her new friends home; Claire seemed happier again and she was doing well in school.

They were waiting for the payment from Canada, and money was always tight. She did not see Nathan often, and twice when she did see him he was with a woman, a nice-looking young brunette from Belgium.

When he made the introductions she could tell that Nathan was watching for her reaction, and she winked her approval. She felt relief somehow, and she was glad for Nathan and the girl.

Once, when he came by to visit them on his own, she said, "What on earth is taking so long with the money? It's been five months already. Did the ship ever leave? Did the wood get there? Look at us here, living hand to mouth. We need the money, Nathan."

"I can see that, Helen. But be patient a bit longer. We should be hearing any day now."

"Can I make some inquiries of my own? Not that I doubt you, but maybe something went wrong."

He said that to his knowledge nothing had gone wrong, but that it was war. "War, Helen. For ships too."

"You keep saying that."

"Because it's true." He stood up. "I have to go. I'll be in Egypt for a while, and then in New York."

More weeks and months went by, and not until the war was over did she finally learn that the ship with all her fortune in wood and sounding charts had never reached Canada. It was December 1918, and she was in a tea room near Oxford Circle with Nathan and the Belgian, and while the girl was in the washroom he leaned close and said that unfortunately he had bad news to tell: the ship had struck a mine and gone down.

"Gone down!"

"Yes."

"Nathan! And? Oh my God!"

"Shh. Not so loud. I am sorry, Helen. I found out just the other day."

"But how? When?"

"A year ago. Soon after it left, near Ramsgate, I'm told." He poured more tea.

"Nathan, look at me. It's all gone, all my money? Is that what you're saying? Just like that?"

"Yes, Helen. The ship sank. Do you need money?"

"Do we need money? Of course we do, Nathan. We're scraping by on what I can earn, but that was to be our safety money, our building-a-future money. You know that."

"If you need money, I can lend you some, I'll be glad to. Why didn't you ever say so?"

"Because we made do. We adjusted and waited. We had the wood money coming."

"Yes, I can see that."

"So that's it? It's all over? All gone?"

"I'm afraid so. I'm sorry."

"And why didn't you find out sooner? A year ago, my God. I thought you had good connections. And the piano factory in Canada, weren't you in touch with them?"

"Helen, does any of that matter?"

"Well, I'm just so shocked. I'm trying to understand."

"I didn't find out sooner because as far as they were concerned the ship was empty when it sank. No troops or war material on board. There was loss of life among the crew, and so they had other things to worry about than the ballast. In fact, for all official purposes your wood wasn't even listed. It couldn't be. I told you that in France."

He sat watching her, and she wanted to weep with disappointment or slap him in anger, but she was too numb to do either.

The Belgian girl came back and sat down. She'd put on fresh lipstick. She had small, pale hands with lacquered fingernails that a man might like to hold but that would be useless on a keyboard. There was a bright ring on the girl's finger that hadn't been there the last time.

Hélène stood up and took out her coin purse. Her hands were shaking. She held on to the table.

"Wait," he said. "Please sit down. I have a proposition."

"Not now, Nathan. I'm so . . . I don't want to hear another word!"

"Please sit down. You are making a scene. What I want to propose is about earning good money fast. Try to calm yourself."

She hesitated, then she sat down again. The Belgian girl looked from one to the other but didn't say anything.

"In a few days I'll be going to Marseille on business. Come with me, and I'll pay you very well. Just a few days. I could use your French, and you'll earn more money in a few days than in years of fixing pianos."

"I do not *fix* pianos, Nathan. You have no idea how Claire and I get by, do you?"

"I guess not. So tell me. How are you getting by?"

"What is going on?" said the Belgian girl. "You would take *her* to Marseille? I speak French."

"I know, but not as well as she," said Nathan. "Hers is the real thing. Yours is more Walloon or something."

"Be careful," Hélène said to the girl in French. "He lost all my money. All of it."

"What? How? He did?"

"Yes. Be careful."

The girl said something to Nathan that she did not bother to hear. There was so much to think about suddenly, such profound disappointment. She felt empty and weak and afraid. She needed to get away and be alone to think this through. She sat for another moment with her purse in her hand and her shoulder bag in her lap, then she put some coins on the table and stood up and left.

Nathan wrote to her twice, suggesting they meet, but she did not reply. She wrote to Juliette, but never heard back. She still gave lessons at the conservatory, but fewer and fewer. She played the organ at two churches for a share of the collections, which was never very much because the Spanish flu had struck and grim posters everywhere reminded people to stay home or to keep their distance and wear gloves.

In the summer of 1919, she and Claire took the ferry across the Channel and then they travelled by train from the French coast. The landscape out the windows was like none they'd ever seen. Everywhere houses and farms and even churches lay in ruin; great flocks of black birds flew up and settled and flapped their wings, and they dragged up bits from the earth and flew off with them dangling from their beaks.

In Montmagny the factory and the house were no more. Only a few walls with great holes in them still stood, and mounds of overgrown rubble lay everywhere. There were signs of large fires: melted window glass and roof and floor beams burnt to the pocket ends. Twisted and burnt machinery. They spent the night at the hotel, which had been rebuilt, and in the light of early morning they looked at their house and factory a second time. They sat on the stone wall by the millrace and moved their hands in the cool water. There were ducks on the pond again. Claire picked some daisies and other wildflowers that had come up through the rubble in the garden, and then they walked to the squire's lodge. It had more broken windows and patched holes in the walls, and the trees all around it were gone.

She was fully struck by this fact only then, all the trees gone, all of them. Just splintered stumps everywhere. One more reason why it all looked so different.

An old man was living in Juliette's apartment, with her furniture. He was white-haired and thin. She remembered him: the sexton, bell-ringer and money collector, with his long pole and velvet sack on a hoop.

She asked about Juliette and told him who they were.

Madame had passed away, he said. In March 1918. He had dug her grave. Just he and the priest had buried her, and since there was no family and the back part of the manse where he'd lived was destroyed, the priest gave permission for him to live here.

The room looked much as it had last time, as though Juliette had just gone out for a moment.

At the church the priest stood counting out sacred hosts from an open box into a chalice. It was still Father Dubert, more frail now. When he saw them he smiled and nodded, and then he locked the box and put it away and went down on one knee and crossed himself.

He pulled himself up with difficulty by the edge of the cabinet and turned to them. "Madame Hélène," he said. He looked genuinely pleased. "And Mademoiselle Claire. Look at you, sweet Claire, how you've grown. You're a young woman now."

He told them that Juliette had been one of Dr. Menasse's last patients before the French army gave him a rank and ordered him to the front. He had not returned. Pneumonia, the doctor had said about Juliette; a kind death if one did not struggle against it.

And her things? she asked. Her clothes and personal effects? Any papers?

"Yes," said Father Dubert. "Her clothes were given away, but there was something."

In the church office he opened a desk drawer and took out an envelope and handed it to her.

"No notebooks or papers?"

He shook his head. "Just this."

On the outside of the envelope she'd written *For Hélène and Claire, with love, always, Juliette.* In it were eight of the old one-franc coins, now quite without value.

Father Dubert saw the coins and he shook his head and smiled.

They walked from the church to the cemetery and put the flowers on her mother's grave. She and Claire sat on an overturned wheelbarrow, and she wiped her eyes and blinked into the sun low over the treeless land, blinked at her mother's name on the wooden cross. The finishing carpenters at the factory had made it from kiln-dried Lebanon cedar to last a hundred years, and they had carved a treble clef into the cross point.

After some time Claire stood up. "Mom," she said. "Let's go."

The last thing they did in Montmagny was visit the magistrate to fill out and sign papers stating that she and her daughter were alive after the war and that she was confirming her title to the war-damaged property, the factory and the house as surveyed and registered in 1809. In the file room the brick wall was still raw with fresh mortar.

~

After the practice session she wanted to try on the finished shoes David Chandler had brought. She led the way to the vestry, and there she watched him take them from his paper bag and set them on the floor: an ankle-high pair for everyday street wear and a lower one for formal occasions.

"French glove leather on these," he said proudly. "Feel how soft, Mrs. Giroux. The toe box is number two sailcloth. From a weaver in Lunenburg."

She put them on and they were wonderful. She took them off and put her hand into the right one to feel what he had done to create such firm support.

He sat watching her. "In the trade we call that a swell, Mrs. Giroux. It should position the foot more firmly. Does it?"

"Very much so, Mr. Chandler. And to be able to do that with shoes that are so soft in other ways. Thank you."

She asked if he was keeping a record of his fees and reminded him not to forget the bookshelf, and he said yes, yes, not to worry. But there was one more very special pair of shoes to come, the ones with a one-and-a-half-inch heel. He said he was using an Italian pattern and that he was working on them now.

"An interesting curve to the heel," he said. "In the Renaissance style." He drew a shape with his finger on the vestry table and looked up at her.

A worn, solemn face, a steady calm. She wondered what William had told him and what his private thoughts were on all this.

"Mr. Chandler," she said from a sudden decision. "It was *frostbite*." She pronounced the word very clearly.

"Frostbite?"

"Yes. You have never asked me, and I thank you for that. I am glad to be able to talk about it now. It'll all come out soon anyway, and I am beginning to see that as a great relief. I didn't think I'd ever say that. People are asking me how I am coping so well, the singers in the choir and Father William, and I tell them it's because this has been hanging over my head for three years. Like that famous sword. So yes, it's a relief."

"You mean facing it again, Mrs. Giroux? Out in the open?"

"Yes. In the past three years, I moved seven times. People would find out who I was, and then reporters would stalk me with their cameras. I believe Father William has told you about my court case and the murder charge. I asked him to. I was acquitted, but now it's back."

"Yes, he did tell me."

"Day after day in that ice hole. I still don't know how many days. Fifteen, twenty. Piano pedals were never a problem, but it took me a long time to learn to walk normally again. And when I am upset I still limp. A bit. Thank you for these good shoes, Mr. Chandler."

fourteen

EARLY IN THE SUMMER OF 1920 she received a letter
from Canada House in London. It said that the Canadian
High Commission was holding a reception for a visiting
minister, and she was invited to try out for the evening's
recital. The note gave a day and a time for her audition.

She went there by taxi and paid with the chit they'd
sent in the envelope. By then she had not seen Nathan in
months, not since the tea shop, and she was surprised to
find him in the waiting room. He put down the newspaper
he was reading and stood up and grinned at her.

"Helen. It's nice to see you again. I gave them your
name, and I hope you don't mind. I know the commissioner, and when I heard about the recital, it was just too
good an opportunity for you to miss. These government
things pay really well. I'll just introduce you and then I'll
leave. How are you?"

"Fine, mostly. No, I don't mind. Thank you."

There was an awkward pause. They were the only people in the room. Nothing but empty wooden chairs on a bare floor, a picture of King George on the wall, and a closed window onto Trafalgar Square. Faint voices through the connecting door.

"I hope you've forgiven me by now," he said. "Having to be the messenger of such bad news. It must have been quite a shock."

"It was."

"Of course. How is Claire?"

"She's doing well. She's settling in better than I am. And you?"

"Fine. I'm just back from Cairo. Marseille went all right, but it would have gone better with you there. And you'd have made very good money."

"Marseille? Oh. Yes."

"Do you want to know how much money you'd have made?"

"Not really."

"As much as two hundred pounds, Helen."

She stared at him. "What would I have had to do for that?"

"Not much. Be there with me as my associate. Smile and speak your best pointy-mouth French."

"Saying what?"

"Nothing specific. Just to put them at ease and let them see that you trust me."

"Trust you? With what?"

He shook his head. "Never mind that now. It's too late, anyway. But in future, Helen. If ever I can help, remember that."

Later she would sometimes feel that there had been something odd about that short conversation; maybe the mention of so much money, or something left unsaid, or perhaps just something about the mood. But at the time she didn't see it. At the time she was more concerned with protecting her inner calm for the audition and with keeping her hands warm.

Minutes later she played for the deputy commissioner and the cultural attaché, and they stopped her halfway through some piece by Cécile Chaminade and hired her.

She decided she'd bring Claire along to turn pages, and the next day she bought evening dresses and shoes for herself and Claire at a second-hand store used by Polish and Russian émigrés. The store was called Verushka's Closet. She spent almost four pounds there, but she knew by then that she'd be getting fully eighteen pounds plus the taxi fare for the evening.

The performance went well, and afterward the minister and the commissioner came up to them where they stood with Nathan and a new girlfriend of his, an English girl, young as well, with blond, curly hair and a pretty face and a good figure. Nathan made the introductions. The minister repeated Hélène's name and asked if she and Claire spoke French.

The next morning a messenger came to the apartment with a request for her to attend another meeting at the High Commission, and just one week later she and Claire were on a special train with the minister and his entourage, visiting European capitals to promote Canada and bring settlers to the prairies.

The minister's name was Monsieur Émile de Fougère. He said he was from Montreal, pronouncing it the French way, *Mon-réal*. He had a full head of white hair and a kind face. He would smile at Claire and call her *Mademoiselle*. When he spoke he sounded the way Xavier had sounded, and both she and Claire liked him all the more for that.

On the train, he would leave his assistants and the newspaper people behind and visit her and Claire in their private compartment; his deputy would knock and ask if it was convenient, and then the minister would enter and sit in the corner place by the window in his vested suit and bow tie and pearl-grey spats.

He carried an old-fashioned monocle in his top pocket, and he would take it out and look over the devastated landscape and shake his head. Hélène told him that her husband, Claire's father, had fallen in the first few weeks. Claire told him about the piano factory and what had happened to it.

"My sympathy, Mademoiselle," he said to Claire. "I lost my older son in the war, in Flanders. He was twenty-eight. He was a captain, but already in command of a company. Usually that takes a major."

"*A captain*," said Claire. "We met a French-Canadian captain. He stayed with us. He was very nice. He showed me how to make animals with my hands. I'd need a light for it." She held up both hands and made a dog's head with one and a chicken with the other.

"A shadow game," said Monsieur de Fougère. He was smiling. "It is called *Tous mes animaux*. My children learned that too. What was your captain's name and unit?"

"We don't know the unit," said Hélène. "His name was Xavier Boucher and he commanded a battery there. In the field beside the factory."

"And he was from Montreal," said Claire.

The minister turned to her. "Would you like me to try and find him, Mademoiselle? Officers can be found. Demobilized soldiers are more difficult, but officers tend to lead more structured lives. I'll see what I can do."

On another visit to their compartment, when they were just an hour from Brussels, he said to Hélène, "I don't know if you are aware of it, Madame, but the war has been disastrous for my country as well. Not only did we lose more than sixty thousand dead and a few hundred thousand wounded, but it has also caused great strife between Quebec and the rest of the Dominion."

"Strife about what? You were helping France."

"True, but that is not how French Canadians saw it. They had no wish to sacrifice their men and their horses for the British Empire, and now they cannot forgive us

[129]

for passing laws that forced them into it. But once we have full employment again, things will calm down."

In Brussels a great circus tent had been put up on a sports field, with areas dedicated to different provinces. Large canvases had been painted with prairie themes and Rocky Mountain views. In a saloon where people could taste smoked salmon and air-dried venison, a man in a leather shirt played a tinny-sounding piano.

The greatest success was the wilderness area, where people could pet a young moose and have their picture taken dressed as Indians and trappers. When the minister discovered how popular the moose was, he had the area where new settlers signed up combined with the wilderness area. From then on, the moose, leggy and much adored, stalked among the people and nibbled at their clothes while a civil servant at a podium assigned 160-acre plots of land on survey maps for less money than she had paid for their second-hand clothes. To the right and left of the platform, farmers stood marvelling at sheaves of wheat with ears of grain bigger and more golden than anyone had ever seen.

At the end of that day there was a reception at the British Embassy. She and Claire, in their finery, gave a recital, and guests in black tie and floor-length evening gowns sat on dainty chairs and sipped champagne.

They travelled on, city after city, collecting immigrants, most of them cast adrift by the war and the end of the Habsburg Empire.

On the way back to the coast, the moose was presented to the Amsterdam zoo as a gift from His Royal Majesty, King George V.

"A successful trip," said the minister to her on the train. "We've been doing this for some time now, bringing them in by the boatload. We lose many in the first year, you see. The land is vast and empty. Thousands of miles from coast to coast. And those prairie provinces, Madame. Nothing but grass and constant wind. After the first winter, many settlers simply disappear, or they die on us. The weak ones do. The strong ones survive and buy out the weak ones for a few cents."

"I so admire your relationship with your daughter," the minister said a few days later, back in London. "Or *envy*, I should say. I did not do as well with my own children. My younger son from my second marriage won't speak to me, and the older one, as I told you, died in Flanders."

This was at his farewell reception, once again at Canada House. It was late September; a warm evening with acacia and maple trees out the windows and fine old buildings golden in the light. Claire had passed her eleven-plus and begun grammar school. That evening, even though she liked Monsieur de Fougère, she had decided not to come along because she had homework to do.

"Madame," said the minister. "You did well for us on this campaign. You and your daughter helped us present cultural and social aspects of French Canada that we did not bring out in the past. I know that you are not from there, but – you understand what I mean. And I've been thinking. Have you ever been to Montreal?"

She shook her head. No, she had not, but she would like to see it someday.

"A fine city," he said. "Considering how new it is. In terms of culture and civilized living, it's by far the best city in the Dominion. Come and visit sometime. I could arrange a concert tour for you and make you and your daughter honorary French Canadians. *Post factum*, as it were. I'll look into it, and I'll cable the High Commission here. I will also be sending a note to the right places to try and locate your captain. Would that interest you, Madame?"

Six weeks later, again at Canada House, the deputy commissioner waved her into his office. He said there had been a communiqué from Monsieur de Fougère's office in Ottawa. The minister had fallen ill, but he had forwarded her name to the Office for Education and Culture, and that office would be pleased to arrange a concert tour for her.

"Cheer them up," said the deputy. "Someone from the motherland coming to their towns. But, the thing is, the flu epidemic was even worse in Canada. I mean, worse than here, for some reason. And it's not over yet. In any case, you'll want to wait a bit. We'll let you know when it's safe to go."

He sat frowning at a thought.

"Hmm," he said then. "There was something else. A message also forwarded by Mr. Fougère."

He searched among the papers on his desk and found it and held it out for her to take. He watched her as she read.

"I'm sorry about the captain," he said then. "The military has taken over an entire hospital in Montreal for those cases. I believe it's called the Sainte Mère de Dieu. Something like that. And some of them do get better."

fifteen

"SHE'LL HANG," Lady Ashley said to anyone who would listen. "Best not get too close to her. She killed a man, can you imagine? Lived in a *cave* with him and one day just murdered him. All of you best stay away from her."

Mildred told her that. Mildred's friendship had been unwavering since that funeral mass for the fishermen when Hélène had improvised the Navy Hymn into a ballad that froze them in their seats and made some of them weep. It turned out that Mildred had lost her father and brother that same all-too-common way, a ship getting swamped in a storm and breaking up in minutes.

She'd asked Mildred if she would please bake a cake for a tea she was planning, and the next day Mildred brought one still warm in a Bundt pan. She also brought a platter to put it on. She put the platter on the kitchen table and turned the form over and tapped it with a knife handle all around.

The cake was perfect: yellow with saffron and dark brown, and glistening with cocoa marbling.

THE PIANO MAKER

"Just for you and Claire to try out," said Mildred. "And it's real cocoa, too. Madame Breton, that's the bank manager's wife, you've seen her at your rehearsals, she gave me almost half a pound of it. If you like it, we'll make another one in time for your tea. Who's coming? Can I ask?"

"A few people, I hope. Including you."

"Oh good. And might David be coming? Is he making shoes for you?"

"Yes, he is. He made these already." She put a foot forward and moved it proudly this way and that.

"Very nice. A good man, that. Was married once, to a local girl. She died with the flu, same week as my husband. No children either, but he has a sister in California."

"Yes, he told me. How old would he be?"

"Hard to say. In his late fifties, but he's a strong man still. Lives in a house that was part of the English fort. The province owns it, and they offered it to him on a long-term lease because of the renovations he's doing, and because a house lived in is better than a house empty."

"I suppose it is. What else did Lady Ashley say?"

"Oh. Don't worry about her. She's just jealous and angry. She had someone in the city look up the old newspapers."

But at the next choir meeting, four of the women and three of the men were absent. She asked Mildred to remind them, and when they did not show for the next practice she wrote out a notice that she would be holding auditions for male and female voices and pinned it to the board.

So many came from up and down the French Shore that she had to make a first cut and a second, and then a third. She kept some for back-up and harmony, and she found a few good voices. The soprano she chose to replace Lady Ashley was the girl with the misshapen cheek from the foundry office. She would need coaching, but she had great promise. By that Sunday the choir was complete again, and because copies of the sheet music for "Morning Has Broken" had arrived, that was the first piece they worked on. One week later she had arranged a solo part and given it to the foundry girl. Her name was Mona.

"Nipped in the face by a horse when she was just a wee one," said Mildred. "A shame, that."

Much of Mona's haunting appeal lay in her courage simply to stand up and sing. And her pure, young voice, lost in all that stone church.

When she gave her tea, she invited Mildred and Mr. Chandler and Claire and Father William. Father William was the only one who did not come; he knocked on her door and explained that it was not something he could do, attend her teas. Not under the circumstances. He said he was sorry and that he hoped she understood.

It was still a good tea. They sat around the low table, and she cut slices from the fresh cake Mildred had brought and served them on the small glass plates from the cupboard. David Chandler had dressed up for the occasion, in a white shirt and tie and a waistcoat and grey sports jacket that all looked brand new but somehow did not quite fit, or perhaps it was simply that he was not used to dressing like that. He talked about the house he lived in.

"There was never a shot fired," he said. "From that fort. Not much left of it now, with the earth berms levelled and some of the walls taken down. Some of them are six rows of brick and stone wide, with sleepers of squared logs to tie it all together."

"I can imagine," she said. "Our town in France was built with stones as well, quarried stone walls everywhere, from the early Middle Ages. It was laid out in a star pattern. People from the universities would come and sketch that main square and the way the streets radiated out."

"Was it much damaged during the war?" said Mr. Chandler.

"Yes, it was. Claire and I saw it in 1919, didn't we, Claire?"

"And not since?"

"No. But I've read that the French government might be rebuilding some of the historic towns."

Mildred asked if the cake was all right. She said next time she'd try mixing in more ground hazelnuts with the flour. They all took a bite and chewed thoughtfully and swallowed and agreed that the cake was very good indeed.

Claire poured more tea for them and offered milk and sugar. It was warm and friendly and not too bright in the room. The sky was going purple, and seagulls were orange specks up high. Hélène clicked on the lamp. There were few silences among them, and in what silences there were she knew that everyone understood that this was an important event for her, perhaps an end of something or a beginning, but an event that might not happen in this way ever again.

Next morning near the end of her practice session, Father William came up to her. She stopped playing.

"May I see you in the vestry, Mrs. Giroux?"

"Now?"

"Yes, please."

She stood up and turned to the pews and said to the dozen people there that practice was probably over for the morning.

In the vestry were Sergeant Elliott and a woman in a wool hat and grey coat buttoned up to her chin. As soon as the door was closed the sergeant said, "Mrs. Giroux, this is our matron, Mrs. Doren. I have been informed by my superiors that in your situation, house arrest is in fact not an option. We cleared a cell in lockup for you, ma'am, and the matron will be taking charge of you."

"Suddenly it's not an option, sergeant? Why is that?"

"I don't know. You can bring a small bag of necessaries, but know that the matron will go through them, and she may reject some of them. Like anything sharp or breakable and anything else like belts or laces or pins. We have to, ma'am. Anything that could be used to harm your person."

They took her there in a black horse-drawn carriage with a single barred window in the door. Through that window she saw people stepping from their doorways to watch them go by. In the carriage the matron sat on one side, she on the other.

"We have just two cells," said the matron. "There's blankets between the cells. I put them up today, so the men can't see in or reach past them to grab you, but they'll try to get your attention. Stay on the far side and ignore them."

The matron sat hunched forward with her elbows on her knees. She said, "He didn't want to do that, the sergeant, put you in the lockup, but the order came direct from the courthouse in the city. Maybe somebody in town complained, or maybe because it's a capital case. I don't know."

For a while they rode in silence and then the matron said, "Almost there now."

In the police station she was led past a cell where three men sat on bunks. They swivelled their heads to follow her, and one started making kissing noises. The matron glanced at her and shook her head and then she unlocked the second cell. The row of blankets hung from a laundry line and against the far wall there was a bunk and a chair and a table.

"Your bag," said the matron. "I need to check it."

The matron emptied the bag on the table and went through the contents. She held up the comb. "I'll have to keep that. Oh, and your boot laces. Almost forgot. And you wouldn't be wearin' a corset or somethin' with long cinch cords, would you?"

"Look at me," she said. "What would I want to be cinching?"

For a while she managed to ignore the men's hissing and vulgar talk. The gate clanged open and the matron brought an enamel jug with water and a cup. She stood by Hélène's bunkside and held out something in one hand. With the other she pointed at her ear.

It was a slice of white bread. Hélène took some and kneaded it and put it in her ears.

The matron was out of her coat now, in a long grey wool skirt and sweater with a braided belt that had a leather truncheon hooked to it.

In the course of the afternoon, Claire came to visit, and so did Mildred and Mr. Chandler and Father William. Every time someone came, the matron let her out of the cell and allowed her and her visitor fifteen minutes in the watch office. That room was heated by a small iron stove, and it had a table and chairs in it. The door had a window on top.

The attorney, Mr. Quormby, was the last person to come that day. He arrived when it was getting dark. He said he'd had to wait for the file to arrive from Edmonton, and then the drive had taken longer than expected because the road was icy in places. He would be spending the night at the hotel.

Mr. Quormby wore a black coat and hat, a white shirt

and bow tie and a grey silk scarf. His face was kind in a way, but it was also set and it gave away nothing.

He took off his coat and hat and smoothed his hair, and then for a moment he stood at the door looking out into the other cell, where one of the men was baring his teeth at him.

"Will you be all right here?" he said. "I'll see what I can do about getting you back into house arrest. Perhaps with more restrictions."

He studied her, taking his time. "Let's sit," he said then. "The bad news is that the charge is first-degree murder with the included lesser offences of second-degree and manslaughter. The Crown will need to prove planning and intent, but first-degree is a hanging offence, Mrs. Giroux. Second-degree is also culpable homicide and it could mean life imprisonment, but there is some leeway for the judge and jury. For manslaughter there is no stated minimum sentence. I'm required by law to point these things out, but I'll say them just this once. Do you have any questions?"

"Yes. What is the new evidence?"

"I don't know yet. But eventually the Crown will have to disclose. Mrs. Giroux, I remember the case in general terms. It interested me then and it interests me now. This evening after dinner I'll look at the file in more detail. For now let me just ask you a few questions."

Sixteen

THAT DAY AT THE Sainte Mère de Dieu in Montreal they'd also searched her bag. Not a matron or a sister but an old commissionaire turned her bag upside down on the desk and went through her things with tobacco-stained fingers.

"Nothing sharp in here, or pointed?" he said. "The first chance some of them get, they do themselves harm. The other day, one lad kept his mother's hatpin and used it in the night. Just keep that in mind, ma'am."

"I will."

"And the young lady?"

"She's my daughter."

"And his?"

"His what?"

"I'm asking is she the captain's daughter."

"No, she's not. But he was very kind to her at a difficult time. She likes him very much."

"If she's not his daughter then she can't go in. She'll

have to wait outside. If she isn't his daughter and she's not sixteen then this is no place for her, ma'am."

"In that case, let's say she *is* his."

"Ma'am. I have no time for that. There's the room down the hall, or she could go outside in the park and wait. You need to wait too, for someone to take you in."

She sat with Claire on one of the wooden benches in the waiting room. The room was over-bright with sunlight and they were the only people in it. On the wall above the door there was a large painting of Mother Mary with her hands reaching out. From somewhere they could hear shouting. Splashing noises. A man screaming.

"While I'm gone, please just wait here," she whispered to Claire. "Don't go out there. I won't be long."

"What are those noises?"

"I don't know. Maybe from baths. Maybe they are still using salt water on the burn cases."

"After all this time?"

"I don't know, Claire. Maybe traffic accidents come here too."

"Is he blind *and* burnt?"

"I don't know. Just wait here for me. Please."

In the end she did not get to see him that day either. A bell began to ring and they heard running footsteps along the hallway and doors opening and slamming shut. Half an hour later the commissionaire came and sent them home.

"But is he all right?" said Hélène. "What happened?"

"Some of them are having a hard time of it."

"Would you at least tell him we were here?"

"He wouldn't know the difference, ma'am."

"And how would you know that? Just tell him, for God's sake. Hélène and Claire from Montmagny in France."

They went several more times to the Sainte Mère, but they never did get to see him. One day when they were there again, another commissionaire wet his finger on his tongue and turned pages in a ledger and then looked up and said that Captain Boucher had passed away five days ago.

"Five days ago? But I was here only last Wednesday."

"Well, ma'am. We lose so many that paperwork can't keep up with them."

In the small park by the hospital, they sat on a stone bench. They could hear streetcar bells, and not far away at a flower stand women bought flowers and carried them up the stone stairs past stone lions to the hospital.

"He was kind," she said to Claire. "And kindness is much underrated. I know you loved him. I did too."

"You think I don't know that?"

She looked sideways at the girl. "What's the matter?"

"I remember hearing you play the piano for him. You sounded different when you played for him. It made me feel lonely. And angry at you."

"Did it, Claire? You never said so."

"Maybe I didn't know it. Or I didn't know how to say it. I can tell you now."

"Why angry?"

"What do you think? I was jealous."

"Yes," she said. "I can understand that." She knew that there was something more she ought to be saying to Claire but she didn't know what.

She had loved that young man. Or needed him as the only hope and goodness within reach and loved him for that. At the time and in that dreadful place. Loved him differently than Claire's father, but perhaps just as much in some ways; that was the confusing truth. Perhaps because of the war. The two of them alone on the blue sofa, as if on a safe island afloat among the madness.

Afterward she'd often wondered if she would have loved him as much and felt that way in peacetime, and now she would never know. Perhaps it would have been just as good. She liked to think that.

In Montreal she and Claire lived in a townhouse in Westmount. Claire had her own room with a white desk that she had chosen herself at Eaton's downtown, and an armoire and shelves and a single bed, all matching. The windows were leaded in the English style, and in the winter months they frosted over thickly and needed rags on the sills to catch the water.

Years went by. In the beginning money was no problem, because the concert swing through Quebec had gone well. For four semesters she taught at the conservatory, but then the all-male, all-English faculty closed ranks against her and her contract was not renewed. And so money did get tight. Half her income was from classes she gave at the Métropolis concert hall on Saint Catherine Street East, and the other half from tuning the pianos for Musique Gauthier, the largest instrument retailer in Montreal. Madame Gauthier hired her because the shop had carried Molnar pianos before the war and had done well with them. But now unemployment was high and pianos were hardly selling any more.

She wrote to a lawyer in Montmagny instructing him to find a buyer for the piece of land where the house and the factory had stood. He wrote back saying he would try, but at the moment there was no market whatsoever for war-damaged real estate.

She had not heard from Nathan since they'd left London; now she often thought of his offer of lucrative work, and she was tempted to try and contact him.

She called Monsieur de Fougère and asked him how hard it would be to find someone who was or had been working for the British government in Egypt.

"Not hard at all," said de Fougère. "The Colonial Service is very thorough in its record-keeping. Would you like me to put in a search request?"

"Not just yet," she said. "But thank you. I'll let you know."

After Xavier's death she'd sometimes wondered why, back in France, Nathan had so firmly dismissed any chance of locating him. Surely some of the Canadian soldiers still there would have known something about a commanding officer who'd just been posted out. And Nathan had been playing cards with them. Had he actually tried? Had Xavier let something slip to some of the other Canadians, and Nathan found out? Had he been jealous? Had he lied to her?

That had been the first time she thought him capable of that, of lying, but at the time she did not pursue the notion. Now she did, and with the help of Madame Gauthier she compiled a list of companies that were making wooden musical instruments in Canada.

There were no fewer than eleven, most with head offices in England or the United States, and she began telephoning them one after the other. To make the calls she went to the telephone exchange on Sherbrooke, and she spaced her visits to allow for the various time zones across Canada. Some companies required three and four calls before she finally found the right person.

"In the late autumn of 1917," she would say. "Or maybe winter. On a ship from England to Halifax and onward from there by rail."

She would listen, and say, "Yes. Perhaps nine hundred cubic feet of fine-grained instrument stock. Winter oak, fruit-tree veneers, and northern spruce. And a roll of detailed placement drawings for harps and soundboards and chamber shapes."

In this methodical way, phone call by phone call, she found out that her wood had in fact arrived at the rail siding of the Cobourg Piano and Organ Company in December 1917. And that a payment of 2,750 Canadian dollars had been made to a bank account in Toronto.

"An account in whose name?" she asked the manager.

"I don't think I'm at liberty to say, ma'am. On the whole it was a well-organized transaction, and it all went exactly as planned. Quite a feat, considering the times. I mean, the war and all."

That night she told Claire what she'd found out.

"He stole it!" said Claire. And then, fiercely: "He lied to you. My God. What a beastly thing to do. How could he?"

"I don't know. But I'm going to ask him. I'll find him, and we're going to get our money."

Monsieur de Fougère's office found Nathan within days, and she wrote him a letter saying that if there was ever another opportunity like Marseille, she would now like to work with him.

Just five weeks later, one evening after dinner, the doorbell rang. She was in the kitchen, cleaning up, and because she knew that Claire was in her room studying, she took off the apron and went to the door. She turned on the outside light and opened up, and there he stood in a coat with the collar turned up against the snow. He grinned and took off his hat.

"It's been a long time, Helen," he said, and he turned and waved to a waiting taxi. The driver put the car in gear and moved off.

Seventeen

WHEN HE'D HUNG UP his coat, she led the way to the kitchen, closed the door behind him, and asked him to sit. There was something different about him, but at the moment she did not care to find out what it was. She took a deep breath.

"Nathan," she said, "you owe us four thousand six hundred dollars. Two thousand seven hundred and fifty plus inflation. I worked it out with the help of my bank manager."

He stared at her. "What?"

"You heard me."

"It's nice to see you too, Helen."

"Yes. That ship never sank. It was the HMS *Labrador*, and it docked safely in Halifax in the winter of 1917."

"What on earth are you talking about?" His face had turned red. "Is that why you wrote to me?"

"Just listen, Nathan. The Cobourg Piano and Organ Company. Mr. John Morland, manager. I spoke with him."

"Helen—"

"You stole from us, Nathan. You lied to us. Knowing full well that I was scraping for money and supporting Claire all these years. *Friends*, you said the day when you came with the trucks and picked up the wood. Shame on you, Nathan. I want that money now, all of it, or I'll report the incident. Monsieur de Fougère has become something of a *real* friend to us. He is well connected in government circles, and he'll help me go to the right places."

She watched the changes in his face, all the colour drained now and then a flicker of something in the eyes – acceptance, she thought. She watched him rub his hands over his forehead. There was grey in his hair now, but the main difference from years ago was in his face and in his posture, in the way he held his head or his shoulders. Guilt? A hint of failure? Could it be? The bold Nathan Homewood suddenly not so sure of himself?

"Are you going to say something, Nathan? An explanation, perhaps. A reason? Not that it'll change anything."

"No. I'm just . . ."

"Yes? Just what?"

"Nothing. You're right, Helen. I was going to tell you tonight."

"Oh, how sweet. Of course you were. Do you know how weak that sounds? Were you going to say you're sorry and that you don't know what came over you? Is that it?"

"Yes. Something like that. I was angry, Helen. When I heard that Pierre had died, I had hopes. That sounds so trite now."

"Hopes for what?"

"For you, of course. For us. He'd been dead three years, for God's sake. I was angry and disappointed and – no, don't say anything, I *was*, and it's the only excuse I have. And let's not even talk about the French-Canadian artillery captain. What was that all about? There were rumours among the men."

"Rumours," she said. "Were there now. Nathan, you remember how that day by the river, when I told you about Pierre, I also told you how I felt about you? Well, nothing ever changed, and we made a deal in France. We shook hands. Friends, we said."

"Yes, we did."

"What you did was shameful."

"All right, all right. Enough. Stop saying it." He looked towards the sink. "Do you think I could have a glass of water?"

She made no move to get up. The word that came to her about him now was *humbled*, and she pressed on.

"I want the money in my bank account within the week, Nathan."

"That won't be possible. I don't have that much at the moment. I can give you a few hundred now and the rest over time."

"Over how much time?"

"I can't say. A year or two."

"No. Not good enough. You'll just have to find a way."

"*Find a way*. It's not so easy any more. Money is drying up and people are going broke. I have prospects, but there are difficulties."

"I don't care about your difficulties. We need our money and I want it now."

"Or else what?" He stood up and reached into his trouser pockets and turned them inside out.

"Oh, stop the theatrics. I haven't told anyone yet, but when I do, Monsieur de Fougère will help me go to the right places. If you don't have the money, then bloody well borrow it. Or sell something."

He stuffed his pockets back into his pants and sat down. "Listen, Helen, please listen—"

"I *am* listening," she snapped. "I'm not sure why, but go ahead."

"All right. Let me tell you how I'm planning to make it up to you. How good is your Vietnamese? You once said you took lessons in Haiphong."

"It's quite good, in fact. I have two Vietnamese piano students. Foreign students are the only ones with any money now. Why do you ask?"

"Because there's some temple art in Can Tho I've been trying to buy. Help me and you can probably have two thousand right there."

"Two thousand dollars?"

"Yes."

"Guilt money, Nathan? Were the two hundred pounds for Marseille also guilt money? Is that why it felt so strange?"

"I don't know what you're talking about."

She got up, filled a glass with water at the sink, and set it before him.

"Help you how?" she said. "Do what?"

"Help me talk to them."

"I know where Can Tho is. It's not far from Saigon. But *temple art* – who would be in a position to sell temple art?"

"The district chief and a French colonial administrator, that's who. The actual site is a day trip into the bush. Fantastic gold carvings of the Buddha and disciples. A grouping of nine or ten figures this high. All for just one thousand dollars. It's a terrific opportunity. I can sell it for five times that much. They have some goodwill money from me already, but these are delicate situations, and suddenly something changed. But it's fixable."

He tried a smile but it failed.

"Work with me, Helen. Like you said in your letter. Did you mean that, or was that just a ploy to bring me here?"

"It was both. Just like I am beginning to see that you have two motives also. To ease your conscience and to enlist my help. But tell me your plan."

"I can give you a few hundred in cash, not this minute but in a day or two, and until the full amount is paid off, I'll cover your expenses and then share my net profits from my deals with you. Fifty-fifty. After that, I'll pay you twenty-five per cent, and we'll sort out expenses case by case."

She sat still, studying this new side of him. "What's the matter, Nathan? What's gone wrong?"

He waved a hand. "Nothing. But like I said, money is getting tight. You must know that. I'm lucky I still have good contacts with a few curators at the big museums. I've just seen one in New York. I know what they are looking for, and I know people in the field. Together you and I could do very well. The things I learned with the EAS."

"The EAS?"

"The Egypt Antiquities Service. I looked after logistics for them. In the evenings we'd be sitting in lounge tents by the pyramids, with our feet up, drinking gin-tonics and tipping our cigarette ashes into golden burial dishes for babies' umbilical cords. For seven years I worked with them, and now I know about field help and transportation and all sorts of things. Most of all, I know what these things will fetch."

Colour was back in his face, and the old Nathan was coming alive. "The money to be made in antiquities, Helen. *The money!* Never mind two thousand – how about *five* thousand in a single deal? Together we can do it. Your language skills, your looks. Good, cultured French opens all sorts of doors. And people trust a man when he is with a woman like you. They trust her and it rubs off and they think he must be a good man if she's with him. Would you like to know a few examples of what's out there? Can Tho, for example—"

"Too far. I couldn't go there just now. Claire still needs me here. I couldn't go away for more than a few days."

"Claire – how is little Claire?"

"Claire is not so little any more. She's seventeen, and she is very well. I told her what you did and she is disgusted with you. She's a bright young woman and she's very strict with me. To protect me from myself, I think. She's at St. Gabrielle's now, in her last year."

"And then?"

"Maybe nursing. But she hasn't decided yet. Or hasn't told me."

"All right. If you can't get away for more than a few days, we could start with something that pays less but is close by. A weekend trip. I happen to know of an opportunity in Quebec City. An Indian agent, but very French. He doesn't trust the English any more than they would trust him, which is a common story here in Canada. So you can see my problem. It's perfect for you, Helen."

He was watching her, and she did not bother to hide her interest. A short trip to begin with. Test him and see how she felt about it. And then gradually more. *Five thousand dollars in a single deal!* You could buy a three-bedroom brick house in Montreal with that. It would pay for all of Claire's education.

"But how can I ever trust you again, Nathan?"

"Trust me? With what, exactly? You're not putting anything in. I'm even paying your expenses. It all hinges on my connections, my information, my deal. What's there to trust?"

"Maybe. And it's all legal?"

"Completely so. I'll make the arrangements."

"And how much money will I get for the Quebec deal?"

"My museum contact will pay me the equivalent of thirteen hundred dollars, and I am paying just three hundred."

"The *equivalent*. In which currency?"

"In pounds, Helen. Your share, if you can help me clinch the deal, will be five hundred dollars."

"Five hundred," she said. It was hard not to smile. "Which museum is that? And what are we buying?"

"A ceremonial mask, and the museum is in England. If you don't mind, let me first see how well you can handle yourself in these situations. Clinch this deal for us and I'll tell you more. Fair enough?"

"All right. What would I have to do?"

"Nothing that doesn't come naturally. Just be yourself. You are my agency associate, my conscience. Dazzle him. Let him see that you trust me, and he will too."

It was a key moment and she was fully aware of it. Yes or no? He was right: what did she have to lose? Sitting in the Westmount kitchen, late evening, with the stove clock ticking and the house so still, and with his hints of outrageous money and the freedom from worry it would bring, she was suddenly ready to give Nathan Homewood and his big ideas another chance.

He must have felt the change in her mood, because his old confident smile was now back in full and he said, "Do you think I could perhaps have some coffee and maybe a piece of bread with something on it? All I've eaten since New York is one lousy hot dog on the train."

"In a minute. Earlier you said you could give me a few hundred dollars now."

"You've become relentless, dear Helen. Yes, I can. I'll

give you three hundred and fifty when I see you at the railroad station. And that's not part of the Quebec deal."

"Three hundred fifty in cash?"

"It's all cash. Always and every time. And Helen?"

"What?"

"*Thank you.*"

She was startled at the formality of that, even strangely moved.

"Would you sign a piece of paper as to what we talked about, Nathan? Agree to your debt and spell out how you'll pay it off? Make it a legal document?"

He opened his hands. "Yes, I would."

Eighteen

IN THE MORNING over breakfast she told Claire, and Claire was shocked. "*Mother!* You are going to do *what* with that man? After what he's done to us. Don't you have any pride? Any dignity?"

"I do have both, Claire. You know very well that I do, and more than some and no less than you. But I also have common sense, and I'm being realistic. Helping him earn money seems to be the quickest way for us to get ours back."

"He stole from us. He lied."

"Yes, he did. He admits all that."

"And? What's his excuse?"

"Does it matter? He says he was angry with me. He had hopes after your father died. He found out about Xavier and he was jealous."

"How ridiculous."

"Is it really? Why, Claire?"

"I don't know. I didn't . . . never mind."

"He wants to make it up to us. Why would I say no? Stop being so cynical."

"He did a terrible thing, Mother!"

"Yes. We know that. And he agrees that he did a terrible thing."

"You see?"

"See what? What would you suggest as the best move forward? Be realistic."

Claire picked up the knife and began spreading butter on a piece of toast.

The Quebec trip came just two days later, on Saturday. Nathan had stayed at a hotel and made his telephone calls, and early that morning she met him at the railroad station. He handed her an envelope, and she opened the flap and looked inside.

She counted seven fifty-dollar bills. Far more money than she'd seen in a long time.

They took the train to Quebec City, and over breakfast in the dining car, while the small villages and church steeples of snowbound Quebec moved past the window, he explained the deal. It was about an Indian transformation mask. He'd seen it. It was a fantastic Mi'kmaq ceremonial thing of rawhide and bones and feathers and mineral paints. The idea of transformation occurred in many religions and cultures, he said. In Egypt they'd found spirit masks of fantastic beings and of eagles and lions. The notion of becoming something or someone else, to slip out of this troublesome life into some kind of bliss, to become something other altogether – even Christianity had that, with the notion of salvation and rising up to heaven, and Buddhism with the promise of getting off the meat wheel. And so forth, he said. In any case, the Indian agent, whose name was Monsieur Jacques Damien, was offering to sell the mask.

"How can he?" she interrupted. "Does he own it?"

"Helen, you are not going to do this every time, are you? He is in possession of it, and it was given to him to sell by an elder of a tribe for the benefit of that tribe. With the money, they can pay their bills at the Hudson's Bay. They can buy clothing, guns, and ammunition. They can make another mask, but they can't make guns. It so happens that I know of a large museum that is building the world's best aboriginal collection, and the curator is an acquaintance of mine. I described the mask to him, without telling him where it is, and he became very excited. We know very little about the Mi'kmaq. About the others in Canada, like the Cree and the Huron, we know a fair bit, but not the Mi'kmaq. The mask is quite old, and it comes with seven pages written by a Jesuit missionary describing the transformation ceremony itself. It's a coup for the museum, and it's a good deal for everybody involved."

Monsieur Damien turned out to be the perfect French gentleman. They met for lunch in the dining room of the Château Frontenac, and throughout the meal he could hardly take his eyes off her as she sat straight-shouldered and interested, with good eye contact and as essentially French as her mother had been on the day of the big sale to the man from Boston. The similarity of the two situations did not escape her, in that both had to do with Nathan and the healing power of money.

They talked about music and France and the devastation the war had caused there. Monsieur Damien had never been to Montmagny, but he'd heard of Molnar pianos, and he shook his head when she described the end of the company.

"But we won, Madame," he said. "We regained our honour, and we built the memorial to Marshal Foch for all to see and never to forget."

After lunch he took them quite unceremoniously to a storeroom in the basement of a government building just one block away, and there was the mask, sitting on a shelf. A dark, moody thing of fur and skin and other materials, dimly lit by an overhead bulb. On the floor, mice stirred and made it hard for her to concentrate.

"I've never seen one like it," said Monsieur Damien. "Along with the pages, it should be the centrepiece of any exhibit."

Nathan gave him three one-hundred-dollar bills from his wallet, and Monsieur Damien thanked him and folded the money and slipped it into his jacket pocket.

"There is a canvas sack for it," he said. "If you look on the floor there, behind you, Madame. Is that it?"

They went back on the night train, with the mask in the sack on its own seat next to Nathan. They had the compartment to themselves and there was only one light on, the one above the door. Out the window the night was deep blue, with moonlight on snow and most of the houses dark.

"You'll be sending me the money, Nathan?"

"Of course. Once the museum has paid me. Or, wait – in this case I can probably do it sooner. I'll call my bank and have them wire it. I'll need the name and branch of your bank and your account number."

For some time they sat in silence. They dozed and woke. There was only the clacking of the wheels and the train whistle at crossings.

"Helen," he said at one time from the dark. "Are you awake?"

"Yes."

"You did well. He liked you. He trusted you, and that made all the difference. There may be situations in the future when you'll need to do more, like help me negotiate or explain."

"Explain?"

"Yes. Ease the way. We'll always discuss our strategy beforehand."

"All right."

When they arrived at the train station in Montreal, it was nearly five o'clock in the morning. They walked to the taxi stand and shook hands. No light in the sky, a damp cold, sparse early morning traffic. They took two different cabs. She held the sack with the mask while he climbed in, and then she passed it to him and closed the door. She saw his face and hand behind the window. She waved back.

Two days later the money was in her bank account. Five hundred dollars for just one day's work.

Nineteen

AFTER SHE'D SPENT THREE nights in jail, the attorney managed to have her released back into house arrest. The matron, Mrs. Doren, unlocked the cell and walked with her to the washroom and stood by while Hélène rinsed her face at the basin. She put on some lipstick and tidied her hair.

"A good man, that," said the matron. "Mr. Quormby. People respect him in these communities. He almost never smiles, have you noticed? And the rare time that he does, it's more like a bite. But what a good lawyer the man is."

The black paddy wagon had been ruled out on an objection to do with prejudice raised by Mr. Quormby, and so the matron sat next to her in the backseat of the RCMP Ford, while the lawyer in his hat and coat sat in the passenger seat and the sergeant was behind the wheel. They drove towards the town centre, past the co-operative and the hotel to the church annex.

For some reason her dreams in the jail had been good.

One night she had even seen her father smiling at her, and he had leaned and reached across a far distance to give her something. She hadn't known what it was, but she'd closed her hand over it and put it safely away in the pocket of her pale-green printed summer dress.

When the RCMP car pulled up, the annex door opened and Father William stood waiting. He wore a coat over his soutane and a flat-brimmed hat on his head. Claire stood off to the side behind him, pale-faced in the dark doorway.

"Here we are," said Mr. Quormby. He turned around. "You understand the new rules, Mrs. Giroux. You are not allowed to have more than one visitor at a time, and Father William is to permit or deny them. He will also be keeping a record of their names and times of coming and going."

"Yes, I understand."

"Good. Please get out now and walk directly to the door. I'll be communicating with you through your daughter, or I'll come and see you in person. Do you need to walk there with her, Mrs. Doren?"

"No, that's all right, Mr. Quormby. As long as I can see her goin' inside and that door closin'."

She turned to Mrs. Doren and thanked her, and she said thank you to the sergeant's eyes in the rear-view mirror. Then she unlatched the door and climbed out into the snow and walked towards Father William and Claire.

~

There had been a day in Montreal when Claire and she had sat at their favourite lookout over the St. Lawrence River, with the fine old buildings in the afternoon sun and all the barges and ships going by. One was a cruise ship, and it gleamed with white paint and glass, and it flew both the Union Jack and the fleur-de-lys. On the main deck men and women in bright clothing stood and mingled, and on a smaller deck people sat at round tables and sipped coffee and champagne. They could see this from the outlook bench, could see the tall flutes catching light and see the mocha cups small in people's hands.

"Maybe think about it some more," she said to Claire. "You finished with good grades and you could study anything you want. Medicine, for instance."

"And we'll pay for it how?"

"Let me worry about that. The trip to Quebec a few months ago with Nathan was an eye-opener, and he's waiting for me to do more."

"No doubt."

"Oh, stop it, Claire. I am earning money again at a time when it's getting harder and harder to do that. Lots of money, with my language skills and my business skills and my social skills. And as for you, a profession like medicine would be the best form of security. A profession is portable."

"Nursing *is* a profession, Mom. And a very good one. I know exactly what I want to do. I've known for some time."

"Sweetheart. Does it have anything to do with the war? Like all the injured at the factory. Or with Xavier?"

"No, it doesn't. Maybe. Does it matter?"

"No, Claire."

"This college isn't as expensive as a top university, but it isn't exactly cheap either. It's one of the best schools in Canada, and it's connected to a famous research hospital in England."

"In England?"

"Yes. I liked it there. I'm even thinking of doing my practicum there. I might have to write some other exam or A levels. I'll find out."

"Isn't the one here still run by the Jesuits? They are a strict order and they have little use for women. I don't think they have a single woman saint."

"Now how would you know that? And even if it's true, it's irrelevant. Jesuits started it, when it was called the Loyola Mission, but it's no longer run by them. It's a hard school to get into, but my grades are good enough. I've already met the head of admissions."

"You have? Claire! You amaze me."

"Well. There's just one thing. It's a boarding school."

"Meaning?"

"Meaning I'll have to live there. Except for one Sunday a month. Then I could come home."

Claire waited. "Mom? Say something. Will you be all right with that? It's what I want to do. You'd be able to go on longer trips with him. Like the one to Saigon. Can Tho. I know you want to go. You loved it in Indochina. We all did. Say you agree."

That fall, with Claire in residence, she began her travels with Nathan, and just one year later his debt was paid off. It was astonishing, the way money rolled in. So much, for apparently so little effort. An office secretary, if she was lucky and still had a job, would have to work two or three years for the money Hélène earned on a single trip.

Can Tho and the Buddhist temple art paid $4,800 after expenses, and half that money was hers. A small fortune, and all she had to do was travel there and learn how to ride an elephant without getting sick or falling off. That took two days at the elephant station. She explained to the handler that she could not squat that way on the animal, not on its neck with her knees widespread behind its ears, and not on a high throne that swayed from side to side. In the end a compromise was reached with a much lower seat and a leather rope for her to hold on to, a kind of rein that looped around the animal's neck and upper legs. The next day, the elephant train set off into the jungle. She still became nauseous and once had to get off the elephant and vomit, but then it went away.

In the village they were met by the district chief and the French regional administrator, and she spoke to them in polite and formal ways; Vietnamese to one, her best French to the other. Over an elaborate meal on a reed mat in his house, the district chief said how happy and impressed he was to hear her speaking his language, and he said that as a result it pleased him all the more to be able to send the culture and art of his people out into the world for everyone to see. And as the dishes were passed around the circle of a dozen people, he said he hoped that the wisdom of Buddha would go in this way from person to person among foreigners, who so far had done nothing other than bring their own laws. He said it was an important cultural mission.

He inclined his head to her and waited while she translated for Nathan.

As a sign of his station, the chief wore a red silk coat that was embroidered with dragons and suns and clouds. His food was being offered to him by two young women who knelt at either side of him.

That night in her own room in a house made of mud bricks and bamboo, she lay under the mosquito net with the window open but the gauze stretched tight and she listened to the noises, distant rustling in the jungle, animals calling out. She lay breathing in the scent of the night and she thought of her family in the little house on Tonkin Hill, of Pierre's face as he knelt on the deck planks of the boat and embraced Claire.

For a while she slept, and when she woke in the night her pillow was wet and she turned it over and wiped her eyes. She lay on her back with her hands on her stomach and eventually she went back to sleep.

In the morning the statues were laid out in a row in the grass, and a holy man in a yellow robe touched them with a carved wand, and then they were wrapped in palm leaves and tied in sacking and loaded onto an elephant. An hour later the train set off on the return journey to Can Tho.

"Wonderful, isn't it?" Nathan said to her during a rest stop along the way. "It's always ceremonial and important, and it's obviously legal and proper by their rules, which are the only rules that count here. Do you see that now, Helen? You and I are merely fortunate to be in the right place with the right connections to give them an opportunity to share what they have with the world."

The Can Tho statues ended up in a famous New York museum; she saw pictures of the display in a prospectus that the museum sent to Nathan. They stood on a stone platform in a dark, cave-like room all their own, lit like a stage play by small directional lamps from above and from the sides: nine figures grouped in veneration around the Buddha. The figures were six inches tall and of solid gold carved in fantastic detail of eyes and lips and hands and regional dress; the museum made it known that they were insured for a million dollars as very early examples of Ma-Xe religious art.

"A million dollars," she said to Nathan at the time. "How much did they pay us for them in the end?"

"They paid us seven thousand. You know that. Take off what we paid for the statues and our expenses, and we were left with four thousand and what, eight hundred? The million-dollar insurance thing is just advertising."

More trips followed.

Usually when they boarded a steamer in London, Nathan would be seen off by a young woman. In the three and a half years of their travels, she met four of them. Pretty and high-breasted they were, with good legs and lipstick and nail polish all of them, but the goodbyes were always overshadowed by tense smiles and unvoiced grievances, and not until the ship had cast off and Nathan could stop waving and turn away did he relax and smile and become the man she knew.

She asked about his women only once, early on. "What happened to the Belgian?" she asked then. "The one in the tea shop. Were you engaged? She seemed nice. And the other one, the blonde at the Canada House concert?"

"The Belgian? Marielle. You drove her off, don't you remember? With the others it was always the same thing after a while. Arguments and differences of opinion. They always wanted marriage and children."

"And that surprised you?"

He shrugged and did not answer. It was the first and last time she inquired, mostly because expressing any interest in that side of his life might have interfered with the complex nature and etiquette of their own relation-ship. Also, she did not really care.

They travelled much of the colonial world in those years; not all the adventures were quite as spectacular as the Buddha statues, but all were unique and interesting, and all were astonishingly profitable.

In one case, Nathan knew of a wooden temple entrance

and altar he could buy in Peru and sell in London; in others, they bought a desiccated Aztec woman holding her tiny desiccated child for Stockholm, and they bought Roman art in North Africa for Vienna.

In one memorable deal, they bought an entire horse and rider, a Kāshān warrior turned to bone and leather in a Persian bog, for a museum in Madrid. On the day when hired helpers were there with block and tackle to hoist the find onto a carriage, the group came under attack from four men on horseback, and it was the first time she saw Nathan reach for a rifle and aim and fire it. She never forgot that. He watched the attackers for a moment and then he reached for the gun and quite calmly stood and fired two warning shots. He watched and fired two more even as the men reined around their horses and took off. The ease with which he did that impressed her, and she told him so.

In the end the shipment reached the museum safely, and one month later the money was in her bank account. By then Nathan's original debt was long paid off, and her share had dropped to twenty-five per cent. But even so, every trip was still a profitable adventure, and it was more than that: along the way, when they needed to rely on each other, a solid peace was made, and eventually they were not just good business partners but also good friends. Crossing the line into intimacy had long ago become unthinkable, and she knew that he understood and respected that. It would have destroyed what they had, and because of that, it too would have been short-lived.

Twenty

UPSTAIRS IN THE ANNEX Claire sat across from her at the kitchen table while they shared lunch. A bit of chicken and wild rice and mashed turnip.

She said, "When did they call?"

"Early this morning. I've looked into the connections already. I feel badly, with the trial coming up. You're sure you don't mind?"

"Well, I'd rather have you here with me, but if you need to go back, you need to go back."

"You've got Mr. Quormby now, and he seems very competent. If necessary I can be back here within a few days. On the Zeppelin, or maybe one of the new airplanes. They're faster across the Atlantic."

"Claire, sweetheart. Please don't worry about me. I'm happy for you. Is it a good opportunity they are talking about?"

"It's fantastic, and it could become permanent after a while. Mrs. Seeley said I did well in the exam. I had to draw a human foot in detail the way a Roentgen tube at three-quarter power would see it from the side. Bones, muscles, and connective tissue. There are more bones and muscles in our hands and feet than in the rest of the body, Mom."

"Are there? I had no idea, Claire."

She got up and collected plates and cutlery and took them to the sink.

Claire said, "I want to spend this last night on the sofa. All right? I'll check out of the hotel and have my bags here when Mr. Chandler comes to get me."

"You could take the bed. I'm sorry that with all this confusion you never stayed here with me."

"Next time. And for tonight I want the sofa, like a sleepover. Do you like him, Mom? Mr. Chandler."

"He is a very solid man, inside. And a fine craftsman. Old-fashioned and polite and considerate."

"Yes, yes. All that. But do you *like* him?"

"I do."

"Mom! How sweet. You're blushing."

"Am I? I'm not."

"Yes, you are. Maybe it's time to put Dad's picture further back on the shelf, or put it away in a drawer. Or let me take it. Come to think of it – that's what I'll do. If you don't mind."

At one time that night she used the bathroom, and afterward she went into the living room to check on Claire. Phosphorescence from the ocean was reflected down from the clouds and in that palest of light Claire lay on her side, asleep and completely at rest. The blanket had slipped half onto the floor, and she picked it up and gently put it back on the girl.

She backed away and for some minutes sat on a chair in the dark room. Then she got up and returned to bed.

In the days leading up to the trial Mr. Quormby met with her several times, and Father William permitted her to continue her practice sessions and take her place again at the church piano. But at the next service Lady Ashley and a few others stood up and walked out, and then Father William in his strong young voice spoke the line from the Bible about casting stones. He said that while there might be some in this community who stood accused of a crime, Christian moral law, which guided basic human conduct in much of the Western world, knew better than to condemn anyone before all the facts were known. And he reminded them that English civil law as confirmed over the centuries said that everyone was innocent until proven guilty.

"Proven in a court of law," he said. "Judge and jury."

It was very quiet in the church when he said those things, but then five more people stood up and with much boot-banging clattered out of their pews and walked away, and the heavy door fell shut behind them.

But on the following Sunday there were many in the church who'd come from other villages east and west along the French Shore, and on the Sunday after that all the pews were full and people stood five deep at the back of the church.

Father William welcomed them all.

"*Oremus*," he said. "Let us pray." And he folded his hands and turned to the tabernacle.

The audience for her practice sessions had also grown, from perhaps a good dozen people to sixty-two on the Friday before the arrival of the circuit court. On that day she and the full choir were working on the Bach cantata for the coming Sunday, the first Sunday in Advent. The cantata was "Now Come, Saviour of the Heathens."

"So many wanting to see and hear you," said Mildred to her afterward. "Row after row, Helen! Like at some concert. I was counting them. It's unbelievable. Some of them were people who must have taken time off from work, like Monsieur Breville who runs the co-op and is our mayor on the side. And Madame Breton was there again, the one who gave us the cocoa. What does that tell you?"

That Sunday for High Mass the church was so full the doors could not be closed. People had come from all over, and they crowded nave and aisles in their winter coats, and they stood in clusters in the street by the main entrance and the side door. The lucky ones caught glimpses of her at the piano as they were performing the "Saviour" can-tata, with the choir grouped on the crossing. At the back of the church and in the street by the west door, they were whispering about it, stranger to stranger. *Is that her?* they said. *Could it really be she killed a man?*

Mildred, with her many sources, told her all that.

A woman called Hermance Beaulieu, who helped out with the church decorations each year, had made wreaths of pine twigs and holly and a red ribbon wound around them diagonally. Hélène bought two of them, along with eight candles, and she gave one wreath and four candles to Mildred and kept the others for herself. Up in the apartment she lit the first candle of Advent.

Later Mr. Quormby came to update her. The prosecutor would be arriving on Thursday, he said. And the circuit court judge, the Honourable Sir James F. Whitmore, was due to arrive on Friday. There would be the usual jury screening and briefing of prosecution and defence, perhaps that same day or the next. And the first day of the trial was set for Monday.

"Good," she said. "Finally."

Mr. Quormby had brought a bottle of sherry and some Christmas cake. As he unwrapped it he said, "If we are going to have a small celebration, is there perhaps someone else you would like to invite? I think that tonight we can make an exception."

"Oh yes," she said. And she counted the names on her fingers.

There was still some light in the sky when they sat on the sofa and the chairs in the living room: David Chandler and Mildred, Mr. Quormby and young Mona the foundry girl, and even Father William, now that the invitation had come from the lawyer.

David Chandler had brought the third pair of shoes, the ones with the Renaissance heel. They were beautiful. Everybody said how nicely they were finished. And that curve to the heel; how did one accomplish that?

There was English bridle leather stacked inside, David Chandler told them. Stacked and glued and pressed and shaped on the ball sander. And fine kid leather stretched over the outside.

She put the shoes on and walked up and down while Mr. Quormby poured sherry.

Twenty-One

AFTER THE BUSINESS WITH the horse and rider in the Persian bog, there was no communication between her and Nathan for some time. The Westmount townhouse where they lived was being sold, and she moved to a smaller place, a two-bedroom fourplex only a few streets away. Musique Gauthier had gone bankrupt in the summer of 1928, and few of her students could still afford classes. But she had money now, enough not to have to worry about it for some time. She'd set up accounts with the Dominion Bank: one for emergencies, another for her own needs, and yet another for Claire's education and boarding fees and pocket money. She bought the Austin motorcar brand new with a cash discount from the dealership and drove it off the lot while the manager and the secretary and the salesman stood waving.

She painted the new flat and some afternoons went for long walks in the parklands and forests around the mountain and along the St. Lawrence River. And every morning she took the trolley to Saint Catherine Street East and used the key they'd given her, and in the room she was still renting at the Métropolis concert hall she turned on the electric fire and rubbed her hands in front of it. Then she sat down and practised the piano.

She knew quite a few people by now, and once in a while she had tea with someone or took them along for a walk or a drive. But she missed deeper, older, more worthwhile relationships; she missed Claire, she missed Nathan. She felt lonely at times, but if anyone had asked her, she would have denied it. She might even have quoted Juliette on the matter, who had lived alone successfully much of her life and had her own strong views on solitude versus loneliness.

But there were the daily breakfasts by herself, the dinners, the same leftover food, sometimes for days. There was Claire's room in the new place with the familiar furniture no longer lived in, and other people's footsteps on the floor above, their dog's nails clicking on the hardwood floor. She considered moving again, to a house of her own, but then did not. At times she even considered returning to France, to Montmagny, to start all over again. She called the lawyer, who told her there had not been a single inquiry about the property.

"In that case, take it off the market," she said. She asked about the prospects for a new piano manufacturing business there now, and he paused a moment and then he said that in his opinion prospects for that sort of enterprise would be poor indeed.

Money meant nothing now, he said. The inflation; beggars everywhere. Had she not heard? Was it much different in Canada? In France a loaf of bread cost more than a skilled worker had earned in an entire day before the war.

One morning when she arrived at the concert hall, the front-office girl handed her an envelope. "A man dropped it off yesterday," the girl said. "Nicely dressed. He said he was looking for you but you'd moved."

It was from Nathan.

In the practice room she took off her coat and read the note twice. She sat down on the piano stool, with the electric fire glowing, and she read it again.

Nathan was in Montreal, looking for her. He had come across a wonderful opportunity. A rare and unusual deal for a very large fee. He needed her.

Deals are becoming fewer, he wrote. *Governments are waking up to the value of their artifacts, but this is a good one. Wait till I tell you. Leave your address with the girl.*

The next evening, he came to her flat for dinner. He brought a good bottle of Bourgogne and two slices of cake from Lennard's. He said he'd just spent a week in New York, and since Montreal was so close he'd taken the train north again and come looking for her. He appeared confident and relaxed, and he was well dressed as usual, in a good suit and shined shoes. There was more grey in his hair now, not at his temples but on top, and somehow that only made him look more interesting. He was aging well, without losing his energy and edge.

"It's good to have a bit of money, Helen. Isn't it? I hope you are putting yours to work. Investing it. With the inflation running so high."

"Investing, now? In these times?"

"Not in the stock market. Something much more clever."

He'd been reading up on paleontology, he said. This new deal was a bit like the Persian horse and rider but more complicated. It would also be ten times more lucrative. He asked if she knew anything about dinosaurs.

"Just what I remember from science in school," she said. "Which isn't much. We read Charles Darwin, *The Origin of Species*. About dinosaurs, I remember that he used them for time-span comparisons. I think he said that they were the dominant species for a hundred million years or more. Then one day they were wiped out. Gone. There was something in the paper not long ago. Someplace out west."

"Probably in Alberta. That's the place for it in the world right now. It's something to do with the last vegetation of a certain kind, and with the soil and the ice shield and then the retreating glaciers that shaved the land down to where it was millions of years ago. We'll let him be the specialist, but we should know the basics. Maybe read up on it a bit."

"What specialist?"

And Nathan told her that one evening in the hotel bar in New York he'd met a man who said he was a claims buyer working for a big oil company. When he found out what Nathan did for a living, he said he wanted to talk to him, not in the bar, where they might be overheard, but out in the lobby.

"And that's what we did, Helen. We sat out there in the leather chairs and there was no one around and this man, Brent was his name, he wouldn't give me his last name or the name of his oil company, but he told me that a geologist friend of his in Canada had just found the entire skull of a dinosaur with a number of vertebrae still attached, and not only that, but with some connective tissue and even scales and skin still covering some of the dome down to the cheeks."

"Is that unusual?"

"Organic tissue eighty million years old? Apparently it's very unusual, but I guess depending on the minerals in the soil, it could happen. Remember the skin of the horse and rider? Tough like saddle leather. He said this find was unheard of and hugely valuable, but the geologist was prepared to disclose the location for money and sell the rights to the find. I asked how much, and Brent said five thousand dollars. Now, wait—" Nathan raised a hand. "I know. It sounds like a lot, and I thought so too. I telephoned my friend at the British Museum, and at first he said that such a find was unheard of. Biologically highly improbable, he called it. But somehow I could tell he was intrigued, and eventually he said that if it did exist it would be an absolute *sensation* in paleontology. His word. I asked how much such a skull with skin on it might be worth, and he said he didn't know."

Nathan paused and grinned at her. "Helen, later that same day he called me and said many thousands of pounds. How many? I said. Twenty, thirty? And he said at least that much. He said that because of the prestige and the international interest, there would be a bidding frenzy among major museums. He called it a once-in-a-lifetime exhibit, and from tissue samples scientists might be able to learn more about dinosaurs and the earth then."

"Amazing," she said.

"Isn't it?"

"Did you talk to that geologist who was selling it?"

"Yes. On the telephone. I had to turn my back while Brent dialled the number."

"And?"

"He's French. *Very* French, and very cautious. Suspicious. That's why I need you."

"Is he here in Canada?"

"I don't know. He clearly knows the value of what he has to offer. He would only say that the site was in northern Alberta. I said I was interested, and he told me to give Brent five hundred dollars' goodwill money just for the contact and to send another five hundred to an address in Alberta. He said he would meet us there, and if he trusts us and we all decide to go ahead he'll want another one thousand up front. Then a guide will take us north and we have to pay him the rest of the money once we've arrived at the site."

"Do you trust the situation?"

"I do. It feels right. That's why I paid the first thousand dollars already. I've almost never been wrong about that sort of thing. But you can see why I need you."

"Because he's French?"

"Yes. And you're good at this by now. This man sounds every bit like the civil servant with the Indian mask, and you'll do much better with his kind than I could. But this time I want you to put up one-half, and then we'll split the profits again down the middle."

"You want me to put up two thousand five hundred dollars?"

"Yes. And cover your own expenses. Full partners this time. It's not as if you're still poor."

There was a long silence while he waited her out. He pulled his cake plate closer and ran the fork over the crumbs and squashed them into the tines and put them in his mouth. He grinned at her.

"What do you say, Helen? I think we can make as much as fifteen or even twenty thousand dollars *each* on this one. And have an adventure straight out of Jack London."

She borrowed Darwin's *Origin* and the work of a modern American paleontologist from the library and read them in a few sittings. She had a last weekend with Claire and told her what she was planning. Claire heard her out and then said, "Keep in mind that this time trust really is an issue. You are risking a lot of money."

"I know. But he kept his word with all the deals we did together, and we now have money because of him."

"But he's cheated you before. Sister Brejon, who teaches psychology, says that people do not change. As they get older they may learn not to repeat mistakes, or they learn to do things more cleverly in order to avoid problems, but their basic nature does not change."

"I'll be watching out for that, Claire. I've learned a few things too."

The Killing

Twenty-Two

THE CIRCUIT COURT arrived in a large Ford motorcar. There was the Honourable Sir James F. Whitmore, the judge, and for his support there were the court clerk and the court scribe and the chauffeur. Soon after he'd settled in at the hotel, the judge called an in-camera briefing of prosecution and defence. The briefing took place in the judge's quarters on the ground floor, in room 101. It was the Royal Suite, the best room at the hotel.

Mildred prepared an elaborate tea, and then she and a maid took the trays there and knocked on the door.

"The three of them were sitting around the table," she said later to Hélène. "There was lots of cigarette smoke in the room, and Sir James is sitting there in shirtsleeves and no collar but with a big wig on his head and white locks down to his shoulders. And Agatha Tancock, that's the assistant Crown attorney, she was smoking and just staring at me with those coal-black eyes."

Mildred said the judge sat waving away the smoke and

she heard him say, "First degree, Mrs. Tancock? You will be able to prove planning and intent?"

And the assistant Crown frowned at the judge and said, "Yes, of course, Your Honour."

Mr. Quormby stood up and opened the patio door to air the room for a moment, and then he helped clear a space for the tea things among the papers and the long gun on the table.

After the briefing Mr. Quormby came to see her, the second-last time before the trial, he said, because he had to drive into the city to look after a few things.

"As I expected, there are notes from the first trial. The judge let us take a look at them, just ten minutes each to keep it fair and even. And by the way, I saw the gun. He had it there as tagged evidence. You didn't say much about it."

"Didn't I?"

"No, you didn't. We'll need to deal with it, and in a minute you'll see why. At the briefing the judge informed us that he's set aside three days for this trial. At first he'll allow time for himself and the jury to learn the circumstances; that's when you'll be describing what led up to the situation, and then the prosecution will introduce the new evidence."

"Have they told you yet what that is?"

"Yes. In general terms. It will have to do with the

testimony of a firearms expert and with the medical report from the hospital. Now tell me about the gun."

"Nathan bought it at the outfitter where we got all our equipment. It was in a small settlement more than a day and a half north of Edmonton by train. Just a few log cabins and dog kennels and that outfitter. I think it was once a trading station of the Hudson's Bay Company. We rented the dogs and the sled there, and we bought supplies. And the gun. Deer Run, the train stop was called. I think I've told you all that."

"Actually, no. This is the first time you mentioned the name of the place. Mrs. Giroux, be prepared to go over it again and again with the judge and the assistant Crown. I have faced Agatha Tancock before. Try as hard as you can not to contradict yourself. Any contradiction and she will not let go of it. That is her trick and it's very effective. Please continue."

"We got there late on the third day after we spent the first two nights at the railroad hotel in Edmonton because we couldn't reach him—"

"Him? Who is that? Try not to use pronouns. Use names and concretia. Be precise. Nothing vague."

"The geologist. We'd left messages at the number he'd given us, and eventually someone called back. But it wasn't him. It was a man called Prosper who said he'd been hired to take us to the site."

"Prosper?"

"Yes. It's an old French name. In French you stress the ending, like Pros-*per*. He was a very good guide."

"But he was not the one who'd found the skull and was now selling it?"

"No. He was acting for that man. We never learned his name. Prosper's job was to guide us there and to take our money. Then he went on his way and we turned around."

"Where was the geologist all this time?"

"We never saw him and never heard from him again. Prosper was the one who called back and told us where to meet him, and early the next morning we took the train north. We stayed in Deer Run for five days, because I had to learn to handle the dogs and the sled. There were two dog teams. Our six dogs and Prosper's three. The cross-country trip to the site took five-and-a-half days. We slept in the tent we'd bought. Prosper had his own. There was snow on the ground but in places the wind had blown it away, and that was where we put up our tents. Native people had camped there before. Prosper could tell from where the rocks lay in circles. Teepee rings, he called them, to hold down the tent skirts."

"Good," said Mr. Quormby. "Do it like that, with as much detail as you can. Was the site marked on any map? Did it have a name?"

"No. There was no map. Prosper simply knew where it was. I heard him use a word one night when we were sitting around a fire making dinner. It sounded like *Atanaskewan*. I asked him about it, and he said it was an old Cree word, something about a river, but not literally since there was no river anywhere near."

"I see. There's something else. I need you to think about how you'll be describing the nature of your relationship with Nathan Homewood. She'll belabour that, and . . . forgive me, but you need to be very clear on that. You both slept in the same tent, and then all those nights in train compartments. She'll be insinuating situations and motives, if only to embarrass you. Think about it and tell me on Monday. I need you to stick to one clear version of the story. The truth is best, because it's most easily remembered. All right?"

She nodded.

"Now tell me about the gun."

"Nathan bought it at the store, along with some boxes of shells. We went into the woods and he showed me how to use it. I'd seen him use a gun in Persia, and I'd been impressed. I trusted him. This gun had three barrels, two side by side on top for shot shells and another below for bullets. It was made in England. Nathan said it was a good all-round game gun. It had a kind of hinge action, and he taught me how to load and select the barrels and how to hold it firmly and fire it. I didn't like using it because of the harsh recoil."

"But did you become fairly competent in the use of it? Loading it, making it safe or ready? Firing it? Considering what happened."

"More or less."

"No. *Did you become reasonably competent with it?*"

"Yes, I did."

He nodded and wrote something down on a piece of paper.

[193]

"Thank you, Mrs. Giroux. Now I would like you to rest as much as possible. Eat well and rest. I'll see you on Monday before the trial."

On Saturday she went down into the church for her usual practice session. She'd asked young Mona and Mildred to attend so that they might work once more on their solo parts in the "Wake and Pray" cantata for the High Mass. Mildred's mature mezzo contrasted beautifully with Mona's young voice. For practice she used the old *répétiteur's* method of having them sing the harmony while she played the melody, and then switch and sing the melody while she played the harmony.

"Be bold," she encouraged them. "Sing from your heart, never from your head. Singing with a single piano is much more difficult than with an organ. An organ can overpower everything, but with a piano they'll actually hear you. You are doing very well."

After the session she found Father William and asked if it was all right for her to have a visitor for tea, and he said by all means, and then she asked Morris to take a message to David Chandler. Up in the apartment she lit the first Advent candle again, and then she dressed for the occasion, in the good wool skirt and top and the shoes with the Italian heel.

By the time he arrived, the sun was nearly down and the light on the tile and thatch roofs and the brick chimneys was deep orange. She brought the view to his attention and for a while they stood at the window. She loved it, she said. It was always different with the changing light, a different mood, a different town almost. The trees and the white seagulls and the sharp texture of the rooflines and the ocean rolling out to meet the sky.

"Yes," he said. "It's beautiful."

While she was pouring tea, he told her he was working on the brass sleeves for the organ components. He described what he was doing, but she was thinking of something else and was not listening.

"Mr. Chandler . . . ," she said, interrupting him.

"Yes?"

"They'll be saying all sorts of things. At the trial. I understand that the prosecutor is a woman who is very good at her job, which is to get convictions. And I want you to know that I'll have no control over what will happen from Monday on. No control, Mr. Chandler. It's quite possible that I lost my mind a bit near the end, in that ice hole. For temporary self-protection, the court psychiatrist said. He had a medical term for it, but I can't recall it now. I wanted to make sure you understood that. They may get me to say things I didn't mean to say; they may restrict me to yes-or-no answers that will skirt all context and turn the questioning in their favour. I'll resist that, but it's still possible that they'll say things that simply won't be true. You will be hearing accusations that . . . in all honesty, Mr. Chandler, what I mean to say is that anything can happen in that court, and it may be fact, but it may not be the truth."

He had been listening to her, looking at her over his cup, and now he leaned forward to put it down in the saucer on the table, very slowly as though it might break or some other thing that was in the room right now might break if he wasn't very careful.

Later she did the dishes and then opened the windows wide. She turned out all the lights and put on her coat and hat and moved the wooden chair into a corner, out of the draft. In the Advent wreath on the coffee table, the candle had burned down into its metal socket and gone out.

She sat in the near-dark with her hands together in her lap. Pierre's photograph was gone from the shelf, and she stood up and rearranged the books more loosely so they took up more space. She returned to the chair.

The windows were still open and there was some light in the sky. Not much. A shimmer, like the pearly inside of some shells she had seen on the rocks.

She sat like this for some minutes and then abruptly rose and turned on all the lights and closed the windows. She took off her coat and hat and then at the kitchen table with pen and paper took stock of everything she had: Claire and this place now; her health and her music and her memories; the gift of having learned in her youth from exceptional people; the memory of the house on Tonkin Hill and the image of Pierre embracing Claire in Haiphong; the beach in Belgium and Claire turning cartwheels;

sitting in the cork room, adjusting and fine-tuning a piano to perfection. The weeks with Xavier.

She looked at the list and tore off the page and put it aside. There was much more, but she did not want to commit that to paper just yet. There was David Chandler's kind and troubled look. There was the support of Father William and the friendship of Mildred, and there was Mr. Quormby. There was the memory of Nathan near the end. There was so much that was good.

But first this.

She looked down at the blank page and began to make herself remember.

~

The dogs had been some northern breed, with shaggy coats and flashing fangs. Males, all six of them, all restless and snarling.

"You need to decide who'll be in charge of them," Prosper said to her and Nathan. "It should be the same person every time. So who?"

"I'd like to try," she said.

The men looked at each other, and then Nathan said, "Good. It'll keep me free to take compass readings and make notes and maps so we don't get lost on the way back."

But Prosper seemed doubtful. "They aren't pets," he said to Nathan. "They're a full working team. If she shows the least bit of weakness, she's lost already. She can whip them and make them hate her, but they'll never submit, and the first chance they get, they'll kill her."

"She's standing right there," said Nathan. "Don't tell *me*. Tell her. Just show her how, and she'll do it."

Prosper did, and from then on her main task in Deer Run was getting the dogs to obey her and accept her as their leader. She put on heavy leather gloves and learned to harness them and then to drive them pulling the sled.

Prosper was a lean man in his forties. He wore rough winter clothing and sheepskin boots and a braided leather lash tied around his middle. He asked if she came from France, and he said his father had been from Quebec and his mother a Métis from Saskatchewan.

"What are the dogs' names?" she asked.

"Names? They don't know names. They know the snap of a whip, and they know the commands and your tone of voice. You've got to be tough with them."

She found it all very difficult at first. The cold, the harshness. The absolute unforgivingness of everything.

Deer Run was an outpost in the wilderness, a tumble of cottages with thin partitions for rooms, and kennels and sheds and the cookhouse and the trading post. The best thing was the bathhouse, where she took many hot showers, knowing that each might be the last for two weeks or more. All these buildings stood in a clearing by the railside; the outfitter, a big, bearded man known as Zach, seemed to be master of everything there. He carried a revolver on his hip, and he collected rent and advised on equipment and weapons. He sold tools and supplies.

When the sun was right they could see the gleam of the railroad track vanishing among the trees. In those trees sat large crows with four-foot wingspans, and they cawed and cackled and rasped, and when they lifted off, branches and treetops shook and shed their snow loads.

The days were sunny but cold. There was a thermometer on the sled, and even at noon with the sun out it said minus four or five degrees Fahrenheit, minus twenty degrees Celsius.

They bought a tent and Arctic sleeping bags and ropes and cooking utensils and better clothing and expedition food preserved in frozen portions labelled *Long Trail*. Nathan bought the gun for protection and also because they would have to supplement their own supplies and kill game for the dogs. Raw meat was all they ate. Nathan practised with the gun, and he made her practise also. After the first few shots she hated it.

"You're not holding it right," he said, and he showed her how. "Firmly pressed into your shoulder pocket. Like this. Watch."

At the end of the second day she lay on the bed in her own tiny room in the cabin, her closet, she called it, nursing the bruises on her upper arm and shoulder with packets of frozen peas.

"Remind me, Nathan," she called through the open door. "Why are we doing all this?"

"For the money, of course," he said cheerfully from the living room. She could hear him feeding chunks of wood into the cannon stove. "And for the fun of it. All this adventuring in fresh air. You did all right in Vietnam and in Persia. This is just a wee bit colder."

She heard him closing the stove door, and then his voice came from around the corner of her doorframe.

"But, Helen . . . can you hear me?"

"Yes, of course I can."

"You do realize that with the French geologist nowhere in the picture, I don't really need you – wait! That doesn't sound right. What I mean is, you don't *have* to stay if you don't want to. But I got you into all this, and now that you're here, I'm glad for your company. It's much more fun together, and God knows there's more than enough money for the two of us."

"I wasn't really asking, Nathan. I'm fine. I really am. But thank you."

There followed more days of learning to handle the dogs. She talked to them and gave them scraps of meat from the cookhouse. She tried kindness, but not too much of it. Once, when the one with half an ear missing turned on her, she leapt back and gave him two lashes, but later at feeding time she watered him and gave him his meat like all the others. She learned to tell them apart and then gave them names. Prosper looked on and frowned but said nothing. She gave them names like Bob, Fritz, and Jack, but then got them mixed up and kept inventing new ones, except for Jack. She always knew Jack because he was the one with the ripped ear. And he was the smartest of the lot. By the middle of the fourth day he stood absolutely still while she put him in harness. She made Jack the point dog, and the others seemed to agree.

They left before sunrise on the sixth day. She harnessed the dogs, and the men packed the sleds. It was minus eleven Fahrenheit, and the air felt like steel. Their breath and that of the dogs rose in undisturbed clouds.

"She'll do all right," she overheard Prosper saying to Nathan, and she liked that.

Thereafter, during the days and weeks that followed, their six dogs were her full responsibility. Nathan rode on the sled and looked after the dead reckoning and the mapping for the return trip, and she fed and harnessed and drove the dogs, standing in the crossboard and strapped in for support between the high runners, the way Prosper had shown her.

It was a wild and free and so very unusual thing to do, and by the end of the first full day she knew not only that she could do it, but that she loved it.

They wore lined parkas and thick wool hats and dark glasses with leather side panels to block the glare from the bright sun on the snow all around, and when the wind came at their faces they wore the felt masks they'd bought at the store. She laughed at the men looking like hooded members of some secret clan, but then of course she looked no different.

The sky was clear except to the west, where distant cloud banks were layering. On the second day Nathan shot a moose and Prosper butchered the steaming carcass into portions to be kept on the sled: one lot for them, one much bigger lot for the dogs.

In the evenings they cooked in front of the tents, simple shelters of canvas sheets snapped together and steepled around an upright pole or a tree and fanned out to rocks or pegs. They ate meat and frozen beans or peas and rice most nights, but she always watered and fed the dogs first with moose meat and moose innards, and every evening she unharnessed them and tied them on individual lengths of rope to pegs or trees away from the sled but close to the tents and the fire.

The dogs lay watching them with their snouts on their paws and the firelight glinting in their eyes.

One such evening Prosper said to her, "You are good with the dogs. They like and respect you. I've seen that only once before, and he was a man who said that animals look at us and they know exactly what we're feeling. Not our thoughts, but our emotions. They read our faces like children, and like children they never forget."

"I believe that. I always wanted a dog when I lived in France, but we never had one. Tell me about the place where we're going."

"Atanaskewan," said Prosper. "The old people say it means, or used to mean, something like *where the river ends*. Except there's no river anywhere near, but there are those stone markers like pyramids. And so maybe it doesn't mean river like a flowing water, but something else that flowed freely and then ended there."

"Like what? Something real or imaginary?"

"To the old people that's just words," he said. "To them the imaginary can be more real than a stone. More than this fire. I've heard of people saved by the imaginary and I've heard of some killed by it. People that know this land, you'd be amazed. They see real things where you can't see anything. I was travelling with a man once, and in the middle of the night he wakes and gets out of the tent because he hears someone calling to him. I got out too, and I saw no one there. But he did. I saw him standing there and talking, and he was not crazy."

The nights were never completely dark, and every night they heard wolves at least once. On each occasion she was awake even before the dogs stood and shook themselves. She crawled out of the sleeping bag and looked at them past the tent flaps and watched them answering back, howling up into the sky. Their breath rose high in the air and the hackles on their necks and backs stood so straight she could see pale light through them.

Early on the fifth day the landscape began to change. There were more trees and less snow, and the ground was rising steadily towards an elevation that was in places bare of snow altogether. At the foot of a rocky outcropping they came across the carcass of a moose. The insides and the top haunch had been eaten and the rest was frozen hard.

"Grizzly," said Prosper. "It's not often you see this and they're rare around here, but see the claw marks? So deep and wide apart? And the strength needed. That's a grizzly."

"I thought bears hibernate this time of year," said Nathan.

"Most do. Not this one, obviously. Or he just woke up and got hungry and had himself a snack." Prosper stood and looked around. "Not far now," he said. He pointed at a pile of rocks in the distance. "See over there? On that rise. The first marker."

"Marking what?" said Nathan.

Prosper ignored that. There was never any doubt that on this leg of the journey it was he who was in charge. He took an axe from his sled and then stood wide-legged over the carcass and swung the axe. Meat and skin and bone came off in hard-frozen chunks.

Twenty-Three

FOR HIGH MASS on Sunday, the church was full again. In all the pews people sat shoulder to shoulder, and they crowded the nave and aisles at the back of the church and clustered again at the open doors.

After the cantata the choir sat down on chairs by the communion rail, and up in the pulpit Father William said, "What is this text telling us? *Wake! Pray!* Is it not telling us to wake up and become accountable for ourselves so that we might be able to rise to our full human and spiritual potential? To live a full life? And to pray for help in achieving it? Is it not saying that help is always at hand because we are children of God, and His spirit and His kindness live within us and all we need to do is allow them to be? To have the courage and the faith to allow them to be. Would that not do wonders for our peace of mind and for the way we see ourselves and others?"

There was not one sound in the congregation. They sat absolutely still and listened to their young, outspoken priest who was so very different in his words and ways than Father McBride had been. Old Bridie, who one Sunday had not appeared in church, and the deputation of church elders that went to look for him found him dead on his bathroom floor with his mouth and eyes wide open as though some terrible insight had come to him in his final moments. They'd propped up his jaw with a piece of soap and closed his unsettling eyes and telephoned the diocese office. Ten days later Father William arrived, down from Corner Brook, Newfoundland. Sullivan was his last name, but after a few weeks hardly anyone used it any more. He was Father William to most, and even just Our William to many behind his back. By then even the old Acadians had already forgiven him that he wasn't from the Shore either. That he wasn't even French.

On this Sunday, with just two more Sundays until Christmas, his congregation looked up at him in the stone pulpit and listened, and in the pauses between his sentences they could hear the wind that had come up overnight from the east, and it sang in the edges of the tin flashing around the windows, and once in a while a particularly strong gust set the bells in the tower resonating, and they could hear them hum, each in its own pitch, like some enormous tuning fork.

After the sermon, while Father William came stepping down from the pulpit, the choir rose from their chairs and they grouped around the piano, and Hélène struck the note for the next carol on the program. It was "O Little

Town of Bethlehem," and after the piano introduction the entire congregation rose and sang along:

> *O little town of Bethlehem,*
> *How still we see thee lie!*
> *Above thy deep and dreamless sleep*
> *The silent stars go by . . .*

~

It was snowing by then, a hard, fast, punishing snow that came nearly sideways and built up quickly against windows and house walls, and the people who had been standing outside the church pressed in more determinedly now, and those for whom there was finally no room turned away and went home or found shelter at the hotel. The skies were dark now and in no time the weather had caused two accidents with horses shying, and then a car with visitors who'd come for the trial skidded at the post office corner into the oak tree there. The snowplow was called out, and the gate to the emergency supply of road grit in the corner by the old gunpowder magazine in the fort was opened.

By Sunday afternoon there were more motorcars in Saint Homais than anyone had ever seen. The hotel was fully booked and the owners of the old Quaker House had come from the city and opened it up, and they'd hired locals to air and heat the place and staff it. By the evening the Quaker was full also and many people who lived in houses with spare rooms rented them out with breakfast. Among the people who'd come to town were the twelve members of the jury. Only one of those was from the north shore; the rest had come from the city and places in between.

The trial and how it would go was the conversation everywhere. And if she was in fact guilty, would she really hang? And how soon after the verdict?

"The last woman on these shores to get the drop was also French," said a schoolteacher from the city to someone as they stood waiting for a table at the hotel that night. "The British strung her and her husband up and pressed their two boys into service with the Royal Navy. During the expulsion of the Acadians. What they call Cajuns down south, in case you don't know," he said in his teacherish way. "They wouldn't leave and wouldn't sign the oath. But it's all so long ago, and a lot of it's probably changed with the telling and maybe never was true."

"Never was true?" Mildred had overheard that, and she turned sharply to him. "You don't know nothin' of what you're talkin' about. You just go up to our graveyard and take a look-see, what this is and where you are now. You want to eat here, you best shut your mouth. For many people on these shores it's what's come down in memory from their own blood, and it's real and it's true. The Americans down in Louisiana and the people in France that took them in and some in other parts of Canada, they'll always be our friends."

That afternoon Hélène had spoken to Claire in London for nearly fifteen minutes. Later she wanted to send a message to David Chandler, but she did not know what that message should be. She had seen him in church and he had smiled and nodded, but after the service, in the confusion of the crowds and the choir, she'd lost sight of him. Someone said something about him having to go home because of the road grit in his yard.

At about seven o'clock Hélène heard someone coming up the stairs, and then there was a thump at the door.

"Your dinner, ma'am," she heard a voice say, and when she opened the door there stood a girl, maybe fifteen, with red curly hair with snow melting in it, and bright blue eyes and a face full of freckles.

"Sorry to knock with the boot, ma'am," the girl said. "My hands are full with this tray. Mrs. Yamoussouke sent me. Dinin' room's full tonight."

"Of course. Come in," said Hélène. "What is your name?"

"It's Marie-Tatin, ma'am."

That night, because the weather was all the other way, she could lie in bed for the longest time with the window open to the trees and the ocean, and she could hear the wind in the trees and the waves on the beach below. Eventually she rose and lowered the window to just a crack and went back to bed. She thought of Pierre and her mother and father and of Juliette, hoping that thinking of them might seed the night and that dreams of them would come.

Twenty-four

ON MONDAY FROM EIGHT o'clock on she answered the lawyer's questions. She watched him taking notes and she listened to his reminders about consistency and the power of detail in a testimony. At nine Mrs. Doren came to fetch her. She put on her coat and hat and the new boots and then walked downstairs ahead of Mrs. Doren to the police car. It was standing in the road with smoke rising from the exhaust into cold air. The sky had cleared and there was almost a foot of snow everywhere, except in the road where the plow had gone through. It all looked so beautiful, so free and wide open. It was so easy to breathe.

"The rear door, Mrs. Giroux," said the matron. "Watch your step there. It's a bit slick."

"I will. Thank you, Mrs. Doren."

They drove to the co-operative market hall and there were cars parked all along the road. Mrs. Doren took her into a side room, where they sat down on upended vegetable crates and waited. They could hear the shuffling of many feet and a man's voice saying "Silence!" And then that voice kept talking. "That'll be the judge," said Mrs. Doren. "He's briefin' the defence and the prosecutor and the jury. It won't be long now."

They listened to the judge for some time, and then there was a pause. They heard him say, "Clerk, bring in the accused."

Mrs. Doren stood up from the crate. "You need to take off your hat now, Mrs. Giroux. And be ready to come with me. I need to be holdin' you by your left elbow."

The door opened, and a man in a black suit and a small white wig looked in.

The market hall was filled with people. At the end where she entered, there was a roped-off area where they'd built a riser for the judge's desk and chair, and on the bricked ground before the riser they'd put more chairs and desks for the scribe and the jury and the lawyers. On the wall behind the judge, a large Union Jack was pinned to the barnwood next to a Red Ensign, and to the near side of the flags were blackboards with the price of produce still chalked on them from the fall. One board said TOMATOES 7¢/LB and another NO DUCKS/CANARDS TODAY.

The jury sat in a row of captain's chairs at a right angle to the judge's desk; a few yards in front and below the judge's desk sat Mr. Quormby at a smaller desk, and not far away at another desk sat a woman with a pale face and black eyes and thin lips. She wore a loose black gown with a white collar, and she sat leaning back casually into her chair. A small white courtroom wig was pinned to her black hair. Probably the assistant Crown attorney.

Behind them in the first row after the rope Hélène saw two Movietones on wooden tripods, and photographers stood clutching their cameras. Everyone was staring at her, and into the absolute silence when the matron made her stand still for a moment, a bright light came on and the Movietones started to grind and click. Flashbulbs exploded by the dozen with a ragged sound.

"Matron," said the judge. And then louder: "*Matron, over here!* Have her stand next to that chair there by her attorney, and you take your position over there against the wall. And that light, someone turn it off or move it. It's in my eyes." He pounded his gavel. "Clerk. Tell them to move that light."

The man in the black suit walked up to the rope.

Mr. Quormby looked different, with a small wig on too. He stood up and leaned close and murmured something that she did not hear because she was taken aback by the assistant Crown's hostile expression and her unblinking black eyes.

The clerk came back and said something to the judge, and the judge frowned and then he hammered the gavel three times down on the wooden plate.

When all was silent the judge read the charge, which was first-degree murder, and he asked her how she pled.

"Not guilty," she said, and the clerk came up and whispered to her to address the judge with *Your Honour*, and she nodded and said, "Not guilty, Your Honour."

The clerk moved her chair to a spot marked with an X in chalk on the brick floor, not directly in front of the judge's riser but to the side a few yards and turned so that she was facing both the judge and the jury. They made her tell the story of how they found the skull, and the assistant Crown hurried her when she took too long with details. The judge had pages in front of him on the desk and he kept referring to them as she spoke, and the assistant Crown kept standing up and asking questions.

~

After they left the dead moose that day, travel became more difficult. In places there was no snow at all, just hard ground. They passed more rock piles, some of them ten feet high with flat sides like pyramids, with dirt and sand blown into the cracks. They wore their masks and glasses because an ice-cold wind had come up and sometimes it gusted so hard it stopped all progress. For long stretches she walked the dogs to lighten the load, now that there was more rock than snow under the runners. The sky was still clear, but to the west the cloud banks had loosened and horsetail clouds were blowing in from the north.

"Over there!" shouted Prosper at one point. "See it?" He pointed at something that she could not make out. They continued over level ground for a while longer, and eventually Prosper stopped and pointed again. "See it now?"

"I bet it's under there," said Nathan. "That sandy hill. I think that's where he found it and then covered it up again. Am I right? Is that why we brought shovels and brushes?"

While the men were at work digging, she fed the dogs and on a solid-fuel burner melted some of the snow she'd packed on the sled for drinking water. The dogs lapped it noisily out of the enamel wash basin. When they were done she stored the basin back on the sled and then sat and watched the men at work.

When the skull lay exposed it came up to her shoulder. It was absolutely astonishing. An ancient bone structure, white in places, with most of its teeth still in place: a row of them, each longer than a chef's knife.

She reached out and tapped the skull, and it sounded hollow. Sand ran inside the bone. There were large holes for the eyes and ears and for the nostrils. Strands of cheek muscles still clung to bone inside their caves, and great patches of scaly skin clung to the skull, brown and dried like old leather, half an inch thick. From the base of the skull the spine curled away, with the large bones fused in places or held together by some ancient and altered substance, as though cartilage had turned to glue and then to stone.

"What do you think?" said Prosper to her. "He didn't find any oil, but he found this."

Lifting the skull and vertebrae onto the sled took planning and then a concerted effort in stages. Even so, the skull was surprisingly light for its size. They didn't cover it for fear of rubbing off precious skin, but they tied it down with ropes, carefully, through openings and over patches of bare bone only.

~

Whenever she paused in her narrative, there was a great silence in the market hall, all these people staring at her. She saw Mr. Quormby like an island of safety not far away. She saw Mildred and David Chandler in the crowd, and she held on to them for support. Flashbulbs still popped once in a while and the bright camera light was off to the side a bit. A piece of cardboard had been raised on a pole to keep the light off the judge's desk, but it was still on her and still an annoyance.

"And then what, Mrs. Giroux?" said the assistant Crown. "Would you please move more quickly and get to the moment when you murdered Mr. Nathan Homewood."

Mr. Quormby stood up and objected, and the judge looked at the assistant Crown and said, "Now, Mrs. Tancock. You know better than that." He turned to the jury and instructed them to ignore that comment because it was prejudicial.

He turned to her. "Please continue, Mrs. Giroux."

"Yes, Your Honour. The sled was a basic platform, and the skull sat in front and the vertebrae were laid out behind it. We tied it all down and then Nathan reviewed his notes and drawings with the guide. The guide made a few comments but on the whole he approved. He said to watch out for the weather. Then we paid him the rest of the money, which was three thousand dollars. We fed the dogs and we all ate something and rested for half an hour, and then we turned around. The guide said he'd be travelling east, but he helped us push the sled clear of sand and rock. Once we were back on snow, we parted. We could see him and his team for another hour or so over our left shoulders, and then we lost sight of him."

~

With the added weight the runners cut more deeply into the snow and the dogs had to work harder. But they were a strong team, and for the rest of that first day it was relatively easy. They simply backtracked the way they'd come, she driving the dogs and Nathan with his notes and compass riding on the sled, and that night they were able to camp at the site where they'd stayed the night before. It was nearly dark when they arrived, and they pitched the tent around the same tree and made a fire.

She fed and watered the dogs, and then they cooked their own dinner. They ate moose meat grilled on the fire. They heated frozen peas and carrots, and they ate coconut cream pie from the Long Trail portion packages it came in.

They joked about things, about how normal people might be spending the evening. They got along so very well by then, like friends who'd been through a lot together; dependable companions on this so-unusual trip.

In the firelight the skull looked all the more strange: those long teeth, the molars as big as an infant's head, the vertebrae enormous and complicated in their structure. Shadows dancing in the eye caves and dancing on ancient flesh in the cheek pockets.

"I took *The Origin of Species* out of the library again," she told him. "Just before we left. Mostly because of his unthinkable time spans. Have you read him?"

"Not recently."

"Well, he says that most likely one day some catastrophic event like a planetary collision wiped out most life on earth and set it back to single-cell forms. And ever so slowly evolution began all over again. It took another seventy or so million years, but this time, among countless branches, one accidental offshoot just happened to have opposable thumbs *and* large brains. Which resulted in the use of tools. And here we are."

Nathan chewed and swallowed and nodded at that.

They mused about their dinosaur being alive, hunting its food, this enormous thing pounding over the land. Those deadly incisors. Surely not just a vegetarian. Maybe an omnivore, if not an outright carnivore. How high off the ground might it have been? How big its feet? Its toenails? How something this big and complicated could evolve from primal mud to dominate life on earth for more than a hundred million years. And then disappear again. Gone.

They heard wolves again that night, and she knelt by the tent flaps and looked out at the dogs standing stiff-hackled, howling back. She loved all this. It was such a privilege, so utterly different from her other life.

Later that night it began to snow. Not very much at first, but by morning when she was harnessing the dogs, snow came down no longer in flakes but in small, dense crystals. They were underway by seven o'clock in a grey, dim light, the kind of light it would be all day. There was snow on their trail now, and at first the dogs could still find their own tracks but by noon they could no longer.

They carried on using Nathan's trail notes and the compass, and they identified landmarks ahead, as far as they could see, which was never very far. From then on they stopped the sled every half hour and decided the new direction.

"Not to worry," said Nathan. "We'll just take our time. So what if it takes a bit longer to get back?"

They travelled like this for seven days.

It was snowing all the time, and they no longer recognized the landscape from his drawings. His dead reckoning notes had become useless as well, because their speed of travel was so much slower than on the way out. But they still had the compass, and guided by it they headed southeast in the knowledge that the general direction was correct.

The snow was dense but high on the ground. The dogs had the large paws of their breed with webbing between the toes, but even so they were sinking in deeply. Often she and Nathan put on snowshoes and helped push the sled for hours.

They did not talk about the fact that they would soon be running out of food, theirs and the dogs'. But they both knew it. And they hadn't seen a moose or any other kind of animal in days.

~

She paused and asked if she might have a glass of water. The clerk brought water, and she drank and handed the glass back to him.

"Your Honour," said the assistant Crown, "can we not go straight to the situation in question? This is a murder trial, not a travel report."

The judge looked at the Crown and then at her. He frowned and looked back at the Crown. "Are you in a hurry, Mrs. Tancock? I think we want to establish the circumstances that led up to the situation in question, as you put it. After all, it's an unusual situation. So let the accused continue. But wait . . ." The judge looked at his watch and said, "Recess. This court will resume at eight o'clock tomorrow morning." He hammered his gavel. "Matron, the accused may be taken back into house arrest. She is not to receive any visitors other than her legal counsel." .

Mr. Quormby stood up and said, "May I approach, Your Honour?" Then he leaned over the desk and murmured to the judge. The Honourable Sir James F. Whitmore reached up and with one finger moved the stiff locks of his white wig back from his ear. He listened.

"Matron," he said then, "the accused may be brought her meals by someone other than her counsel."

She and Mr. Quormby were in the apartment when Mildred came up the stairs with a tray. "Meatloaf," she said. "I'll put it in the kitchen. And there's red cabbage with apples and honey, and mashed potatoes and gravy. Food to stick to your ribs, Helen. You'll be needing it."

"Mrs. Yamoussouke," called Mr. Quormby from the living room. "Can you tell me? What is the feeling among the people in the gallery?"

Mildred stood in the doorway to the kitchen. "Behind the rope, Mr. Quormby?"

"Yes. Behind the rope."

"I wasn't there all the time, but from what I've seen I'd say it's very good. People are listening. I think they're sympathetic. The clerk should give her an elbow chair like the jury, not that uncomfortable straight-back to sit on, why don't you tell them that?"

"Because it's courtroom protocol. Other than that?"

"Fine, Mr. Quormby. I think she's doing very well, don't you?"

"Yes, I do think so. Thank you, Mrs. Yamoussouke."

Twenty-five

ON THE EIGHTH DAY of the return trip, the snow stopped coming down in the late afternoon, and when the air in the distance had cleared they saw an elevation and a rock pile that according to Nathan's notes and sketches weren't supposed to be there. They took a compass reading and the needle veered wildly, and when it settled it told them they were heading west-northwest.

"How is that possible?" said Nathan. "How on earth? What's going on? We've been travelling mainly south and a bit easterly the whole time." He took another reading, and the heading was the same: 290 degrees west-northwest.

"What now, Nathan? Do we know where we are?"

"Give me a minute and I'll tell you."

The dogs stood in their traces and looked back at them with their tongues lolling. She melted snow and watered them and then melted more to fill the flasks.

While she worked, Nathan sat on the sled studying his

notes. He kept aligning his drawings with the compass and adjusting the bezel.

When she had finished with the dogs, she sat down next to him and he told her that for some reason they'd been going in a wide left-veering circle, and that the elevation in the distance was the sandy hill where they'd found the dead moose on the way out.

"And that rock pile?" he said. "It's the one he pointed out from the other direction when we came up to the carcass. I'm sure of it. Except that now we're looking at it from the east, not from southwest."

"A circle. How is that possible?"

"I don't know. Maybe compass deviation. Or magnetic outcroppings, iron ore. I read somewhere about the seven-day circle in some northern latitudes. The good news is that the weather has cleared, and so from now on we can go by the sun and my watch. And there's something else: we're not far from that moose carcass. We could get the rest of the meat. It'll be frozen solid and should still be good to eat. So you could even say we're lucky. We know again where we are, and we'll just forget the compass and head southeast by the sun."

"You're sure, Nathan?"

"I am, absolutely."

"All right. So let's head for the moose. There was a lot of meat left on it. The whole underside. Can we still make it today?"

"We can try."

She went to the front of the team and led it around, and

then they headed for the elevation. To her left the sun was one hand above the horizon, and the sky and all the air around shimmered with ice crystals. She walked next to Jack in her snowshoes, talking to him, cheering him on: *Come on Jack, I know you can do this. Good boy, show them how it's done.* And Jack leaned into the traces and sometimes, looking sideways at him, she could swear he was laughing.

Where the snow was not so deep, she stopped the dogs and took off her snowshoes. She climbed on the sled and stood between the runners and drove them in the singsong voice she'd learned from Prosper.

They reached the foot of the hill in less than an hour. They could see where the dead moose would be, halfway up the elevation, on that ledge. By now the sun was below the horizon and it was getting dark quickly. Ahead it would be all sand again and difficult travel.

She stopped the dogs and talked about it with Nathan. Should they continue or should they make camp here and get to the carcass in the morning?

"We have enough meat for tonight, and the dogs are tired," she said. "Maybe we should do the hard part when we're all fresh and then head back."

And so for that night they simply threw the tarpaulin over the sled and tied it down and then slept in their Arctic bags like mummies next to the skull on the platform. They heard wolves again and the dogs howled back. At one point Nathan climbed out of his bag and pulled the gun from its sheath. He knew she was awake.

"We don't want them eating our moose," he said. "I'll just go take a quick look and scare them off."

She heard him struggling with the frozen tie-downs on the tarp, and then he slipped out the opening and she could hear his footsteps moving away.

~

That was what she told them on the second day of the trial. The hall was filled again, and the light and the cameras were on her. This time several items lay on a harvest table that had been set up for the day's proceedings next to the desk of the assistant Crown. Expert witnesses for the prosecution were waiting in the side room.

She sat on the same chair, but they had given her a glass of water on an upended vegetable crate nearby. The judge seemed quite taken with her narrative and he had cautioned the assistant Crown twice already not to interrupt, especially not with prejudicial comments.

She was less than an hour into her testimony when she said, "That was when it happened, Your Honour. I heard him walking away and maybe thirty seconds later there was a very loud sound, like a shot almost, a sudden loud crash, and then I heard Nathan screaming. I'd never heard anyone scream like that, like a huge curse and a scream with such escalating terror. I got out of the bag and grabbed the flashlight and climbed off the sled. The dogs were all up and howling, and I pointed the flashlight and maybe twenty yards away I saw Nathan on the ground, but in a strange twisted way. He was still screaming but his voice was getting hoarse, and by the time I got there he lay with his eyes and lips pressed closed . . .

"A heavy metal thing with teeth had grabbed his leg. That thing was so strong, the teeth on it had gone deep into his leg above the knee from both sides and broken the bone there. Blood spurted out thick and fast. I could see this with the flashlight, and I ran back to the sled and got some rope and then I tied off his thigh above the injury."

The assistant Crown stood up and said, "At this point I must ask the accused a few questions, Your Honour. We have the very object here: it is a number four O'Grady bear trap. It is illegal now, but until one year ago it was still being used. Mostly for large bears in western Canada. I would like to ask the accused now why she did not simply open the trap and free Mr. Homewood from it."

"So ask, Mrs. Tancock," said the judge.

"Thank you, Your Honour. Mrs. Giroux, why didn't you just open the trap?"

Hélène looked at Mr. Quormby and he nodded. He seemed pleased with that question.

"I tried, but I couldn't," she said. "Mrs. Tancock, I'd like you to try and pull those jaws apart with your hands. Try it now."

There was suppressed laughter in the audience and the judge said, "Quiet! Mrs. Giroux, please just answer the question."

"Your Honour, I did try to pull the jaws apart, of course
I did, but it was impossible. I couldn't even get my fingers
under them. The wolves and the dogs were still howling,
and I think I was panicking with the horrible injury and
all the blood, but I did use the flashlight to see if there
was another way to open the trap. I could not find any.
There was blood everywhere. Blood had gushed out, and
even after I'd tied it off it kept pulsing down his leg onto
the trap and his boots, and it froze there."

"Your Honour," said the assistant Crown, "I would like
to call my first witness now. Would the clerk ask Mr.
Samuel Merrifield to come in and stand on that marked
spot at the other end of Your Honour's desk."

The clerk looked at the judge, and the judge leaned back
and raised a hand and made the motion to proceed.

The clerk brought in a lean old man with white hair and
a tanned face. He wore a black suit and black boots and a
white shirt with a collar and a black string tie with a silver
bead. The clerk showed him where to stand, and he held
up the Bible and had the man put his hand on it and repeat
the words of the oath after him.

"Mr. Merrifield," said the assistant Crown then, "what
is your profession?"

"I'm a fixer, ma'am. Was a trapper until last winter, but
now I mostly repair things. Traps and tools to do with my
old line of work."

"Mr. Merrifield, please come closer and look at this trap
here. Pick it up and show us how it works."

The old man walked to the table and looked down at the trap. It was a massive thing of black iron and a chain and thick springs linked to the jaws where they were hinged to the frame. He dragged it off the table with visible effort and set it on the floor. For a moment it was all very quiet, and then the chain slid and rattled off the table and fell heavily onto the brick floor. At the end of the chain was a solid piece of iron hammered into a three-pronged grapnel hook. Mr. Merrifield looked over his shoulder and said, "That there is called a drag, ma'am. It catches on bushes and rocks."

The judge leaned forward across his desk to see. "My," he said. "Go on, Mr. Merrifield."

The old man knelt on the floor and brought his face down close to the bottom of the trap. He stood up again. "There's a sear on the underside, kind of like the sear in a gun lock but much heavier, and with this trap when more than thirty or so pounds of pressure comes down on the plate, it releases."

"But now that it's closed, how do you open it?" said the assistant Crown.

"Well. With the weaker ones you could use a spring clamp and reset them, but then these O'Gradys came along, and this one has four springs with a good eighty pounds' pressure each. So they put a slip release under the base plate, and with that all you needed to do was hit it hard."

"Would you please show us?"

Merrifield put the trap on its side. "I'll see if I can kick it open." He gave the underside of the trap a good kick, and the trap skidded a short distance across the floor but it did not open. Merrifield lined it up again and stood and swung his boot, and with the second kick there was a harsh metallic sound and the trap leapt up and then relaxed. When Merrifield stood it upright, the jaws fell away to either side.

"That didn't seem to be very difficult, Mr. Merrifield," said the assistant Crown.

"No, ma'am. Not if you know how and you get her sweet spot."

"Could one not learn that from studying the mechanics to see how they work? They are openly accessible."

"Well, ma'am. I suppose so."

"Thank you, Mr. Merrifield." The assistant Crown seemed pleased. "I have no further questions, Your Honour."

"Your witness then, Mr. Quormby," said the judge.

Mr. Quormby stood up and said, "Mr. Merrifield, have you ever seen an animal caught in one of these traps?"

"I never have, sir. But I've heard of it, out west. A few times, in fact. Couple of times a grizzly, and another time a cow. Broke all the bones and held fast to muscle and sinew."

"A cow? With the release under the trap and not so easily accessible for a good kick like you've just shown us, how do they release the trap with a heavy animal in it?"

"They wouldn't, sir. They'd kill the animal to get to the underside of the trap and kick it open. Better still, use an axe. The blunt side of it."

"I see. Kill the animal and then use an axe on the trap. And if a man were caught in it with his leg broken and it's deep-freezing temperatures, and let's say there's blood and frozen snow clumping on it, could that mechanism freeze?"

"Well, I suppose it could."

The assistant Crown stood up and said, "Your Honour, he is leading the witness."

"No more than you, Mrs. Tancock," said the judge. "Carry on, Mr. Quormby."

"Thank you, Your Honour. Mr. Merrifield, and if it's in the snow in the middle of the night and you don't know that there is such a mechanism, and a man is caught in it as we've just heard – how could one release the trap then?"

"Well, sir. I wouldn't know."

"If the jaws were closed, could you pull them apart, Mr. Merrifield? You, with your hands?"

"Sir?"

"Could you personally open the jaws of this trap with your hands, Mr. Merrifield?"

"Against a more'n-three-hundred-pound pressure? I could not, sir. I doubt that any man could. You'd need a horse and chains to do that. Or machinery. A pulley system would do it. Settin' them was dangerous too. That's one reason they're not allowin' that trap any more. That, and the damage it did to the animal."

"Thank you, Mr. Merrifield."

~

That night, blood kept seeping from under the tourniquet. She fought to control her panic, and eventually she managed to steady her hands and to refashion the tourniquet with loops at either end, through which she put a tent peg and then twisted it as tight as she could and locked it with the sharp end under the rope. She brought the tarpaulins from the sled and improvised a cover over them with walking poles to keep the canvas up and breathing holes where it did not meet the ground. Basic cover, and it would have to do for now. It was dark under there, and the smells of his blood and vomit were strong. She went back to the sled and brought the spirit burner. The thermometer on the sled said minus ten degrees Fahrenheit. Back at the tent she set up the burner next to the crawl-hole and melted snow.

She talked to him as she cleaned his face and soaked up the vomit with snow. He did not respond. She shone her flashlight on him and put her cheek close to his mouth to feel his breath. She wondered if she should cut off his trouser leg to see to the injury. There was a small box with basic medical supplies on the sled. Iodine. Gauze. Tape. Scissors and Band-Aids.

Dear God, she said. *Please help me now*. She would always remember this, reverting back to a child's prayer in fear and helplessness. *Please, God, don't let this be as bad as it looks*. But in clearer moments, when her panic allowed any thought at all, she knew that it was. The bars of the jaws that gripped him were as thick as her arms, and the teeth, as sharp as chisels, had broken bone and cut an artery.

Near morning it began to snow again, not the soft snow of mild weather but hard crystals that clung to the tarp and to the skull on the sled when she walked there to check on it.

In the thin grey light of morning she watered and fed the dogs. Just half a day's meat left now. Jack was watching her intently; she feared he was reading her mind, the black turmoil in it. "It's all right," she said to him. "It's all right." He lifted his nose and sampled the air and looked at her again.

In the tent Nathan woke and passed out and woke again. For brief moments he seemed to regain a sense of control.

"Go to the moose," he said. "Get the rest of the meat. Collect clean snow and pile it by the entrance. And then bring the first aid kit and whatever else we might need from the sled."

The moose carcass was a one-hour hike from the tent. She reached it by mid-morning and saw that something had been eating at it. The wolves. She stood over it with the axe and chopped through hip and shoulder bones into the underside of it and put the chunks in a canvas sack. She left the axe there and dragged the sack back to the sled.

At the tent she made a kind of seat in the snow for him, with snow for a backrest and a blanket that she pushed around and under him for insulation. She melted snow and made soup and spooned it into his mouth. Chicken noodle soup with frozen peas in the Long Trail packages.

He said, "Helen, I want you to cut the trousers around that spot and soak it with iodine. Then keep me covered with my sleeping bag. I'm freezing and burning up at the same time."

The lower part of his leg below the jaws was blue-white. She daubed on iodine and wrapped gauze around where the teeth had sunk into his flesh.

That day went by, grey and cold, and the night. The wolves were back. Morning came and it was still snowing, that same persistent blowing snow that kept piling up and drifting and piling up. She looked after the dogs, watered them, fed them. They had dug snow holes for themselves and they lay curled up in them, nose to tail, blinking at her as she turned away, back to the tent.

"There must be something we can do," she said to him.

"There is, Helen. We can wait. Somebody will come. Trappers walk their line." He closed his eyes. His lips were pulled back, taut, chapped, bleeding. There was a freezing sweat on his brow and his teeth showed, bared to the gums. He grimaced with pain. "Are you sure we don't have any morphine in that box?"

"I'm sure, Nathan."

She looked again at his leg, and it was now purple around the knee and calf but the ankle and foot were turning black.

At some point on the third or fourth day he said, "Where is the gun?"

"I don't know."

"Go look for it. I had it with me to scare the wolves away. It can't be far. It's loaded, so be careful."

Twenty-Six

THE COURT RECESSED again, and when the matron took her outside to the car there was a second movie camera set up in the street. Photographers stood waiting. A reporter with a microphone called to her and asked for a few words for the Pathé company but the matron, who was gripping her elbow, said sternly, "Madam can't talk now. Don't be pesterin' her."

Lunch that day was a stew, and she was only half finished when Mr. Quormby arrived. She put the stew in the wall larder and sat with him. He told her she had done well. "The judge sees you as credible, and that is very good. Never exaggerate, and if it feels wrong, don't say it. Be careful treading the line we've decided on. Never speak to impress. But you know all that."

He told her to rest as much as possible now, because the next day would be the most difficult. He said he had a good feeling about it all, but the judge had told them that he had allowed only three days for this case. It was a circuit court, he said, not some higher court where they could take months.

When he had left she opened the windows in the living room wide and stood at the one that looked out onto the roofs and the street, stood in the draft feeling the cold air on her face. She closed the windows and put on her coat and went down to the church to ask Father William if she could call Claire.

"Yes, of course," he said.

In the office she pulled the coat tighter and then moved the desk chair to the telephone and called the long-distance exchange. In London she spoke to someone else but eventually Claire was on the line, and after the first few words her eyes filled and her heart ached. It was Claire's voice, just Claire being there and wise in her young ways and knowing better than to prod about how the case was going.

"Are you all right, Mom?"

"I am, Claire. I'm fine."

"You want to tell me?"

"Oh, Claire. I think it's going all right. I don't know."

There was a silence in the phone while Claire waited for her to say more, and when she didn't Claire said, "You'll tell me when you want to. Listen, I'm on the short list for the position! There'll be one more interview, but I'll know before Christmas. And maybe then I can come over again. This time I could try Imperial Air. There's a service to New York on an airplane. It's a bit more expensive than the Zep, but it's quicker. You won't mind?"

"Mind? You mean the money? Oh, Claire, sweetheart. No, I don't mind. Just use whatever we have. I'd love it if you could come."

She wiped her eyes with the tissue in her cuff. "Claire," she said, "I do think it's going well. That's what Mr. Quormby says. And Mildred too."

Afterward she went back upstairs for a long nap. She took off her clothes and put on her nightgown, unpinned her hair and washed her face and closed the drapes on the bedroom window. She lay back under the cover and closed her eyes.

She considered praying, as she had done often in that tent. Prayer containing the words *please*, *God* gave the illusion of hope and of someone caring. It took her away from there. She remembered her despair and his stillness and sudden frantic gasping, the sickening odour of his leg. More vomit: his, and some time later her own.

She sat up in bed and waited for her heart to calm. She went into the bathroom and brushed her teeth and crawled back into bed.

~

She'd gone to look for the gun. She'd paced the area around the tent and poked in the snow with a stick. When the trap closed on his leg, how far and in which direction might he have thrown it? In what sort of involuntary movement from shock and surprise? She wondered if there might be a second trap somewhere, and she prayed that there wasn't.

"I can't find the gun," she told him.

But he was not conscious. She looked at the injury, and the thigh too was now turning black and swollen. Perhaps the tourniquet was too tight. She loosened it and black blood pulsed. She tightened it again.

She knotted herself a kind of harness with ropes for the sack, and then she hiked up again to the carcass. But there was hardly any meat left on it. She could see the paw prints and tooth marks of the wolves, where they'd crunched the spine and scraped away the meat down to the inside of the hide. She swung the axe and chopped out what was left of the bones and cracked the skull and made three trips with the sack filled with bones and hide. It took from early light until dusk.

This was how the next few days passed, she might tell them in court tomorrow. She might begin to skip certain details. Such as the fact that when the dogs had nothing left to eat but bare bones chewed over and over, she briefly considered melting the snow with Nathan's blood in it and feeding them that. It was possible she was beginning to lose her mind then. When the air in the tent became unbreathable, she would crawl out on all fours and vomit and wipe her mouth with snow and crawl back inside. She made herself a small breathing hole where the tarpaulin met the ground, and she'd lie in her sleeping bag with her nose close to the hole.

At times he sang with his eyes closed. She remembered that so well, how for some reason it had made her flesh crawl all the more. The hopeless, empty, croaking voice in the darkness.

He sang "Waltzing Matilda." Then he sang "Spanish Ladies." *Adieu and farewell to you*, and when the words would not come he would groan and croak the melody, and curse and pass out and wake and pass out.

She lost count of the days. She was so exhausted she was beginning to crawl to see to the dogs rather than walk.

One time he woke with a scream, and he kicked and the trap rattled. "Go find the gun," he pleaded with her.

His face looked horrible, ghostly and thin and white with blood smears on it, and unshaven, with tears frozen on his cheeks. "Helen, I'm begging you, go find the gun. It's out there. I'm full of poison. Look at this. Black. Stinking. You know what that means."

She searched methodically with the stick, and this time she found it. It was down in a crack between rocks. She poked it out, mindful of the trigger. She looked for the safety and pushed it on, and then she cleaned the snow out of the muzzles and hid the gun under her sleeping bag. He had passed out again.

At the sled she found the last package of peas and the last rice, and she cooked the rice and then put in the lump of frozen peas. She shook him awake and spooned warm mush into his mouth. She ate some herself and followed up their meal with a portion each of Long Trail coconut cream pie, hard as stone. Nathan sucked greedily and chewed and swallowed, but then he vomited it all up again. She wiped his face and his lap with snow and threw it out of the tent.

"I saw you hiding the gun," he said with his eyes closed. "You need to shoot me and then carry on. In the heart, because the head's too messy. There, I've said it. Listen, Helen, I'm of a clear mind at this moment. Never been clearer."

"Nonsense, Nathan. Here, drink some water."

"No. Listen, Helen. Have the courage. Do it and leave while you and the dogs still have some strength left. Maybe you'll come across some game."

She said nothing to that. Nothing. She heard him and did not object. It was the crossroads. Killing him was suddenly thinkable. A mercy death for him, survival for her.

She leaned forward and kissed him on the cheek. On her lips she felt the blackened and broken skin on his cheekbone above the weeks-old beard.

He turned his head and looked at her in surprise.

"Helen," he said then. "Dear Helen. Please hear me. They won't find us in time. I was wrong. How is the weather now?"

"Ice haze. Very cold."

"But can you see the sun?"

"At times."

"So just head southeast by the sun and your watch. I showed you how, remember? Leave, Helen. But help me with this first."

His eyes were round and feverish, no spark left in them now, only emptiness and terror. He reached out with one hand across the steel trap that stood up in their tent like some hellish anchor that held them fast to this place. "Helen, in the heart. Here!"

He unbuttoned his parka and the coat underneath, and the shirt. He tore at the buttons and with greedy fingers ripped a tear into the shirt. And with the same fingers, thin and dirty, he paced off his chest. Three, four down; one, two left of the sternum. "Right here," he said. He spoke with fresh hope. "Look! Here. Are you looking, Helen? I am making a scratch-mark for you. A bullet or a shot shell, it doesn't matter. I will close my eyes. I'll hold the muzzle, you pull the trigger. Make the decision and do it, hard and fast."

He was weeping now, pleading.

"Helen! Do it! Do this one thing for me. You owe me. I saved your lives in France. You *owe* me, Helen. Help me now!"

~

She got out of bed and opened the blinds. She walked into the living room. What time? Just past four o'clock. The sun was nearly down and the roofs stood unevenly against the sky; shadowed light on old ridge tiles, snow on thatch and cedar. Smoke rising from David Chandler's chimney, straight in the air. No wind. Not snowing now. She went back into the bedroom and closed the blinds and stepped barefoot into the fine shoes he'd made for her. She sat down on the bed in the dim light and lay back for a moment. She lay with her hands covering her face. *How to live with all that? How to tell it? How?*

Later she went into the kitchen. She sat in the chair and looked down at her feet in those beautiful shoes with the Renaissance heel. Fine leather, neat stitching. A pattern there on the side.

She took the leftover stew from the wall larder and ate it with her fingers, three fingers forming cold lumps and putting them into her mouth and letting them melt there to slide down. *Thank you, my Lord, and will you please forgive me.*

Marie-Tatin, the young kitchen maid with the red curls and the freckles, found her asleep at the table, her cheek in the crook of her arm.

"Ma'am!" cried Marie-Tatin. "Goodness me, ma'am." She quickly put down the dinner tray and stepped closer. She helped her sit upright and raised her up from the chair. "Ma'am, let's get you to bed. You want to eat later? What a day you must have had. Come this way."

Twenty-Seven

IN THE MORNING the Honourable Sir James F. Whitmore began the proceedings by reminding defence and prosecution that the case had to be brought to a close that day. He said, "Mrs. Tancock, now that we are familiar with the situation, I would ask you to move on to the fresh evidence that this retrial is based on. Please proceed."

The assistant Crown rose from her chair and held up some pieces of paper. "Your Honour," she said. "I have here copies of a medical report and of the sworn testimony of one Mr. Tom Cutter. Both were presented at the last trial, but it seems to the Crown that certain key points that were dismissed must now be seen in a new light. In the course of my questioning and presentation of evidence, I will be connecting a number of aspects to support the charge of first-degree murder."

"So go ahead, Mrs. Tancock."

"Your Honour, Mr. Cutter is a trapper, and early one morning that December he was out inspecting his trapline when he saw some dogs or coyotes, in his words, in the near distance. One of the dogs came charging his way and he almost shot it, but then he noticed that it had on a body harness. The dog came right up to him, and it kept on barking and turning away in a northerly direction. It stood and watched him and barked, and when he did not follow, it came back to him. In his words now, 'I know dogs, and this one was trying to tell me something and lead me somewhere . . .'

"Because of the harness on the dog, Mr. Cutter eventually followed it, and by late afternoon the dog had led him to the tent, and in it he found Mrs. Giroux and Mr. Homewood. I will now read the key sentences from his statement. He says, 'I found the woman only half under a sleeping bag, curled up in one corner, and I thought she was dead. The man was on a kind of snow seat and he was obviously dead. His right leg was in a bear trap and he had also been shot in the chest at close range. There was a great deal of blood everywhere. I knelt and touched the woman and she was not all cold, so I shook her and she stirred, and when she saw me she blinked and covered her face. I looked around for a gun but could not find one in the tent. Not far away there was a sled, a wide-runner Templeton 6, that's a freight model. There were no dogs but the traces were still attached. There was snow on the sled, and one big domed object, and when I scraped away the snow and ice from some of it I saw what looked like a very large fossil. Other than that, the platform was mostly empty. Near the sled

I tripped over a gun that was lying in the snow. I picked it up and saw that it was loaded in all three chambers, and I made it safe and put it in the box on my sled. I prepared food from my own supplies and I gave the woman some warm broth. I hitched the strange dog into my own team and then I carried the woman to my sled. I covered her and tied her down and then I took her to Silverdale, which was four hours east. It was night now, but with snow on the ground it's never completely dark up there, and I know that country real well. There is a hospital in Silverdale, and I took her there and then I went and talked to the RCMP. They kept the gun, and in the morning they organized an expedition to the site and I came along as their guide.'"

The assistant Crown held up the pages and said, "Those are the words of the first witness on the scene. *Prima facie*, Your Honour. I now have some questions for Mrs. Giroux."

For a moment there was an enormous silence in the hall, as if all the people in it weren't daring to breathe or stir. Then a camera flash went off, over-bright and loud, and the judge blinked and pounded his gavel. "That photographer – now, wait a minute. Clerk, I want you to clear this court of all cameras and any device that keeps a record of any kind. There will be no pictures and no film taken from now on, and no recording machine is allowed. See to it, clerk. And have them take down that blasted light while you're at it. Sergeant and matron, go help the clerk, and if these picture people give you any trouble, arrest them and throw them in jail. We'll just sit here and wait."

There was a commotion and muted protests, but it was all over in minutes, and then a much softer light in the room came from the windows along the west side and from the overhead light bulbs in enamel shades. Out the windows it was snowing again.

"Well," said the judge. "Proceed, Mrs. Tancock."

The assistant Crown stood up and looked at her. "Mrs. Giroux, were you and Mr. Homewood lovers?"

"No, we were not. We were travelling companions and old friends. He was running a business in museum exhibits and he wanted my help, my language skills. I helped him."

"You helped him. But were you also intimate, Mrs. Giroux? I believe this question was not asked at the last trial, but I have my reasons, Your Honour, as we shall see."

Hélène looked at Mr. Quormby, but he just shrugged and opened his hands.

"Intimate?"

"Mrs. Giroux, did you have sexual relations with the man? That is the simple question."

"No, I did not."

"Night after night in a tent. Travelling as a man-and-woman team, and you were never intimate?"

"No, we were not. We were friends. There are some good friendships that sexual relations can only spoil. We met years ago in France when he had business dealings with my mother. In time we developed respect and a liking for each other."

"As friends?"

"Yes."

"Does friendship preclude sexual relations?"

Mr. Quormby stood up and said, "Objection, Your Honour. Would my learned friend like to move on from that point. Her question has already been answered in the negative. More than once."

"So it has," said the judge. "Move on, Mrs. Tancock."

"I shall, Your Honour. Mrs. Giroux, how were you intending to feed the dogs after you ran out of meat?"

"I had no clear plan for that. I was in shock. I was preoccupied with Nathan's injury."

"I'm sure you were. But is it not true that you felt sorry for the dogs too? You've told us how you came to understand and handle them, and suddenly you couldn't feed them any more. They would have starved to death, and so you set them free. Is that not the case? We know that at least one of them was still in a harness. Would you please stand up, Mrs. Giroux."

She rose and then stood there for a moment where the X marked her spot, and she closed her eyes and took a deep breath. She opened her eyes and said, "Yes. I did set them free."

"Ah. Thank you! You did set them free! You did, and in doing so you also sealed your own fate. Because you knew that now you would not be able to leave that place, and you accepted that. Yes? Because is it not also true that after a number of terrible days or weeks in this tent – as it's being called here, but really it was just a mean crawl space under a tarpaulin held up with sticks – is it not also true that after all those hopeless days of suffering and before you set the dogs free, you and Mr. Homewood made a murder-suicide pact, Mrs. Giroux? You were to kill him and then take your own life. Is that not true?"

"No. It is not."

"It is not?"

"No."

"Very well. Your Honour, at this time I would like to bring in my second witness. Would the clerk please ask Mr. Christian-Jones to come in and stand here at this table."

The clerk brought in a man in his forties with blond hair, wearing an English shooting jacket. He was sworn in and then the assistant Crown said, "Mr. Christian-Jones, what is your profession?"

"I'm a stock-fitter, ma'am. And a gunsmith."

"What does a stock-fitter do?"

"We work on guns, especially shotguns, so that they fit exactly. We shape the stock to fit the shooter so the gun comes up just right."

"And do you also know about gun locks and gun barrels?"

"I would say I do, ma'am. I have a master's brief from the British guild of gunsmiths."

"Thank you. Would you take a good look at this gun here on the table and tell us about it?"

The gunsmith picked up the gun and hinged it open and checked that it was unloaded. He raised it and sighted through the bores towards the windows, and he turned it in the light to see details on the receiver and barrels.

"It's a very good gun, ma'am. And a rare configuration, a double-over and single-under. This one was made in England by the firm of Bentley and Barnes. It's an all-round gaming gun with two smooth bores for shot or slugs, and one rifled for bullets. The barrels are relatively long for the model. Thirty inches, I should say. Because of their independent locks, these guns are favoured as the first gun on expeditions in the colonies."

"I see. Mr. Christian-Jones, could one kill a man with this gun?"

"Kill a man – yes, of course one could. They are twelve-gauge barrels for shot, and the rifled barrel is bored and chambered for a big-game shell and bullet. Those bullets are mostly round-nosed and solid lead with no jacket because they hit harder that way. Fired from this gun, a bullet would develop tremendous muzzle energy. Inside the target, say in a body of muscle and organs and bone, a lead bullet with that much energy would deform instantly. It would cause massive tissue damage. That is why it's used for big game, ma'am. You could drop a grizzly with that, first shot. And a twelve-gauge at close range would tear out a man's entire heart in an instant."

"I see," said the assistant Crown. "And if the rifle were fired at a man's body at close range, say from a few inches away, would the bullet go right through? And what would it look like on the other side?"

"It would pass right through, ma'am. Instantly. On the other side, a lead bullet might look like a sheared lump as big as this fingertip. I've also seen them flat like a coin, but if it fragmented you'd find only pieces of lead."

"Thank you, Mr. Christian-Jones. Now, tell us, could a person kill themselves with this gun?"

Once again there was a deep silence in the hall. The crowd behind the rope barrier stood mesmerized, staring at the gunsmith and the gun in his hands.

She had sat down again on the chair, and she sat with her eyes closed. She did not care what they thought about that. Sat unmoving with her eyes closed and her hair pinned up neatly, in the dark-grey wool dress with the creases almost all hung out, and silk stockings. On her feet she wore again the good new outdoor shoes David Chandler had made for her.

And since she sat with her eyes looking inward now, she did not see what the gunsmith was doing. Mildred told her later how he held up Nathan's gun with both hands and turned his head to look at the assistant Crown. "Kill themselves, ma'am? Is that the question? How a person might accomplish that?"

"Yes, Mr. Christian-Jones. That is the question. Move on, please. We don't have all day."

"Well, ma'am. It would not be easy. A thirty-inch barrel, plus the length of the receiver. I do not know anybody with arms long enough to hold up this gun and put the muzzle to his head or in his mouth or to his chest and still be able to reach the trigger."

He demonstrated, and with the muzzle at his face, his probing index finger came well short of the gun lock. He set the gun butt-down on the floor and said, "But if they are desperate enough, they'll find a way. I've heard of people using a stick to push the trigger, but more often than that they'll use their bare foot."

He lowered his forehead to the muzzle and raised his right foot from the ground. "The large toe, ma'am," he said. "The bare large toe in the trigger guard. That is how they could do it."

"Thank you, Mr. Christian-Jones. I have no more questions, Your Honour."

The judge looked away from the demonstration, and he shook his head once as though to dislodge some unwanted thought inside it. He looked at her sitting there with her eyes closed, and he sat back and said, "Your witness, Mr. Quormby."

Mr. Quormby stood up. He, who was usually so calm and confident, now seemed confused and troubled. He stood thinking of what to say – you could feel that, said Mildred later – and then he told the judge that he had no questions for this witness. "Not now," he said. "Perhaps later, Your Honour."

The gunsmith was shown out of the hall by the clerk, and the judge gave the jury members a long look and then he nodded at the assistant Crown and told her to proceed.

And the assistant Crown stood up. She was smiling. "The accused seems to be asleep," she said. "Would she please open her eyes and pay attention?"

Hélène obeyed, and the assistant Crown said, "Thank you, Mrs. Giroux. Your Honour, as to the new evidence now that was previously not linked with the murder, I am asking the accused to please take off her right shoe and remove the stocking on that leg."

She waited, then continued: "Mrs. Giroux, would you please do that now, and then stand up and raise the hem of your dress so that this court may have a clear view of your bare right foot."

Twenty-Eight

SHE NEVER TOLD HIM that she'd let the dogs go. She'd stumbled away from the tent and gone to talk to them. They rose in their snow holes and nuzzled her hand looking for food, but there was none left. She'd already chopped off some of the last vertebrae from the skull and given them to the dogs; how removed from reality she must have been already to imagine that the dogs might accept an eighty-million-year-old bone as food. She had watched them sniff as they might sniff a stone and look back up at her.

When she unshackled them from the trace lines, they shook themselves, and they took a few steps away and stopped to look back at her. They raised their noses and sampled the air for directions of scent. And then when she waved her arms at them, they took off. Only Jack did not. He stood and looked at her, and he bounded away almost playfully and came back.

"Go!" she told him. "Go, Jack. Please go." She waved her arm in the direction the others had gone. Already they were mere dark spots in the distance. "Jack," she said, and she went down on one knee. "Don't look at me like that." She held his head with both hands behind his ears. He tried to pull away but she held him. She put her nose close to his and said, "Go, Jack. Please go now. Leave."

She straightened up and waved her arm with the same throwing-away motion. And he took one last look at her as if to make sure, and then he ran off.

In the tent Nathan was still breathing, but his face was a grimace pulled apart with steel hooks and then left that way. The smell of rot from his leg was thick and damp like a fog. They'd eaten the last of the Long Trail food, rice boiled with the last soup cube.

He woke and moved his lips and said, "Water." He saw her and said, "Helen, you're still here. I thought you'd left."

She held the cup to his lips, which looked as if they'd been cut with a dull knife and had never healed. "Drink," she said. He tried to, but most of it ran down his chin.

She looked out the tent and there was nothing. No future, no past, just an everlasting emptiness. Snow and ice fog and the end of another day with another horror night to come.

He had passed out again. She sat and picked up the gun, and it was so heavy she could hardly lift it. She raised one knee and rested the gun on it and leaned away from it and put the stock to her shoulder. She wished she were dead herself.

His clothing had shifted over the mark he'd scratched for her on his chest, and she put down the gun and crawled forward and with both hands picked apart the tunic flaps and the two other layers of fabric underneath, down to the scratch on his white skin.

She backed up on hands and knees and sat and raised the gun again. She clicked off the safety and hinged open the receiver to make sure there was a shell in it. There was. She moved the selector to the lower barrel and raised her knee and rested the gun on it. And then slowly she crabbed forward and forward until the muzzle covered the mark over his heart.

She closed her eyes and pulled the trigger. The recoil slammed into her and her ears rang, and with her eyes still closed she dropped the gun and patted the ground for her sleeping bag and covered herself with it.

Please, God, she said in the darkness.

~

Now she stood away from the chair, and they were all staring at her naked foot. All except for the people who perhaps cared for her. Mildred in the front row and Father William and David Chandler not far away were looking at her face. Young Mona the foundry girl, with her hand covering her mouth, was too. And Mr. Quormby was. Even the strict and honourable Sir James F. Whitmore had glanced down at her foot only briefly, and now he was looking into her eyes.

But the assistant Crown had the stage and she stood feasting on this, pointing with her index finger. "Mrs.

Giroux," she said in mock surprise. "What happened to your toes? How did you lose them?"

She looked down and raised the hem of the dress right up to her knee, and then she backed away and sat on the chair and started on the stocking. She rose and turned to the wall and rolled it up all the way and straightened the seam. She slipped shut the two garter clips and stroked down the hem.

"Mrs. Giroux," said the assistant Crown. "I asked you a question."

She ignored that while she stepped into the boot and sat on the chair to lace it up.

"Your Honour," said the assistant Crown. "Shall we remind the accused of the meaning of the term *contempt of court*?"

But the judge waved a hand. "You are not the court, Mrs. Tancock. I am. Let her get dressed."

With her shoe back on her foot she looked at Mr. Quormby, and he opened his hands wide and nodded at her as if to say, *It is time*.

The assistant Crown said, "Mrs. Giroux, I have here the medical report from the hospital in Silverdale, and it says that the three outside toes on your right foot had to be removed due to necrosis from acute frostbite. How did that happen?"

"It happened because I took off my boot and socks on that foot in order to operate the trigger on the gun. Exactly the way the gunsmith told you. I heard him."

"'In order to operate the trigger on the gun.' Now wait, Mrs. Giroux. Are you telling us now that you *did* want to kill yourself? After you'd unshackled the dogs and shot Mr. Homewood, you wanted to do away with yourself also?"

"Yes," she said. "I did."

"*You did!* So you did shoot him. Did you?"

"Yes, I did."

"At the beginning of this trial you were asked how you pled to the charge of murder, and you said 'not guilty.' Are you changing your plea now? Would you please speak up and repeat for the record what you just said. That you were trying to kill yourself after you shot Mr. Nathan Homewood. Are you admitting to us now that you did murder the man?"

"No. Helping him die was the most difficult thing I have ever done. It was an act of kindness."

"An act of *kindness*? Hear, hear! Are you mocking us, madam? 'The most difficult thing.' Is that perhaps because you did have a lovers' pact, a murder-suicide pact, with the man after all?"

"No. Because we had been through so much together and I'd come to know him so well, I did love him in a way, but not in the simple way you keep suggesting."

"Whatever that means," said the assistant Crown. She stood savouring the moment. "Well, thank you. Your Honour, in the previous trial in Edmonton, the gun was dismissed because it had been found well outside the tent and had been handled by the trapper and by the police. Also, because it was still loaded in all three barrels and no bullet was ever recovered, it could not be proven that this was the gun used in the murder. Also, the accused's injury was not connected with attempted suicide. In addition, the memory of the accused was impaired, and she was judged mentally unfit. Your Honour, the prosecution now submits that today's expert testimony and the confession by the accused are proof of her guilt of murder in the first degree. I may have more questions for her later, but I have none at this time."

The judge had been using one hand to cup his ear under the wig; now he took that hand away and turned his head and looked out the window. People followed his gaze to see what he was looking at, but there was nothing to see. Those were industrial-grade windows of untrue glass with old wire mesh on the outside, and because it was snowing again, all one could see was the wire and the rust on it and snowflakes coming down and settling ever so gently on the wire.

Eventually the judge turned and made a motion with his hand. He said, "Proceed, Mr. Quormby."

Mr. Quormby stood up and said, "Mrs. Giroux, you told us you were intending to kill yourself. And yet you are here with us today. What happened?"

"I tried," she said. "I knew that the rifle was now empty but there were two shot shells in the chambers. I put my forehead to the muzzle and I pushed with my bare toe, but the second trigger did not work. I remembered about the safety and I clicked the barrel selector forward and back, and I opened the breech and closed it. I tried again, but the gun would not fire. I dragged it to the sled and looked for more rifle shells, and I did find some. I put one in the breech and closed the gun. I stood in the snow by the sled, but when I tried to raise my foot to put my toe to the trigger, I could not do it. It was as though some power other than myself were holding down my foot and would not allow it. And then, as I stood there, it was as if I could see myself and all my life until then, and the tent and the sled and the gun from above, and what I was thinking of doing seemed so irrelevant and wrong in all this solitude. An eighty-million-year-old skull on the sled, Mr. Quormby. And without even thinking about it, I dropped the gun and turned away from the sled. There was snow and ice everywhere. I crawled back to the tent, and I must have been simply too shocked and maybe numb with cold to put that boot back on. I talked to him, but he was dead. I was glad for him. I thought it was my duty to stay with him and to wait until someone found us. I know that by then I was not myself any more. I do not remember much after that."

"You were glad for him."

"Yes, I was. And I was relieved that I had found the courage to help him. He'd been dying in a terrible way from the injury. The entire leg had gone black. His gums and his tongue and lips were a deep, cracked black, and there were black spots on his face. He had been begging me for days to help him end his life, and finally I'd been able to do it."

Mr. Quormby waited for a moment and then he said, "Is there anything else you wish to tell the court?"

"No. Not really. What I did was so difficult I lost my mind over it. Right then, and for a time afterward. You have the report from the hospital and from the asylum in Edmonton. It was not murder, Mr. Quormby. I know it in my heart. It was the right thing to do. It was an unbearable act of kindness."

The Honourable Sir James F. Whitmore asked if there was anything further from prosecution or defence, and there was not. The assistant Crown was first to address the jury. "She confessed," she reminded them, and then she built her argument around that fact. Mr. Quormby came second. His address was much shorter.

Afterward the judge dismissed everyone in the hall except for the jury members, who were told to sit and wait for their instructions. The people filed out, all turning their heads at her, and the assistant Crown picked up her files and strode away.

Outside there was a mob of reporters and photographers. They shouted questions and snapped pictures. The matron held her elbow and steered her past them to the police car, but Mr. Quormby stopped and faced them. He told the reporters that the jury would now be deliberating. There would be no news until the verdict.

At the RCMP Ford, Mrs. Doren got behind the wheel

and Mr. Quormby sat in the backseat with Hélène. At one point he put his hand on hers and left it there for a moment before he took it away.

It was late afternoon by then, and lights had come on in many of the houses. The snowplow had been through and the road was clear, but there was only one lane. A great deal of snow had been banked against the cars alongside the road.

In the mirror the matron's eyes were on her. "You need to stay in your apartment, Mrs. Giroux," she said. "Until I come and get you, whenever that is. Mr. Quormby, you can stay with her, but no one else. All right?"

A room for the jury's deliberations had been prepared at the hotel, rooms 202 and 203 with the connecting doors folded wide open and several tables pushed together. Mildred and Marie-Tatin carried up trays with dinner and pots of tea. The special that night was venison in a mushroom sauce with a choice of side dishes. The court clerk in his black suit and with his wig still on sat on a chair outside the jury room door. He'd ordered the venison with white-bread dumplings and green peas from the valley. He ate from a tray in his lap, cutting up the food and then switching hands and eating with the fork while listening to the noises in the room, the clatter of plates and cutlery and then less and less clatter but voices, some of them louder than he felt they ought to be.

Marie-Tatin came up and collected his tray. "How's it goin' in there?" she asked him. She stood there in a halo of red hair under the ceiling light in the hallway, holding the tray against her hip.

"It's going quite well, I think," he said. "Is there any dessert?"

"Oh, sure. You can have puddin' or the apricot compote. Which would you like?"

"What kind of pudding?"

"Chocolate," she said and smiled at him. "And it's real milk, not powdered."

"The pudding then," he said.

"What are they talkin' about in there? Can you hear?"

"I'm not supposed to. My job is to make sure the door is closed and they don't get out."

She brought him a generous serving of pudding, and while he ate he let her stand by the door and listen.

"Which one is that?" she whispered.

"I wouldn't know her name. She's the jury foreman. They all have one vote, but she's in charge."

"Oh, her. That's Mrs. Fitch. She's the postmistress from down the coast."

In the room they were arguing. "But she killed him," a man's voice said. "Doornail-dead. She said so herself. A woman picks up a gun and shoots a man dead, is that not murder? It would be, the other way round. What is there to waffle and go on about?"

The foreman's voice said, "Please, Mr. Dunsmore. We

need to proceed slowly and deliberately. Someone go to the criminal code and read section eighteen to us again . . ."

The clerk ran a crooked finger inside the pudding bowl and licked it. He put the spoon in the bowl and held it out for Marie-Tatin to take. "There. You should go now. Can't have anyone see you standing there, listening."

The jury deliberated until nearly nine o'clock that night. Then the foreman declared an impasse and invoked her option to bring in the judge for counsel.

The judge had been in his room, reading the file and dozing and waking. He'd had Mildred make him a pot of coffee, and he drank it all and went to the bathroom twice while he waited.

When the clerk knocked, the judge said, "Come in," and then he listened to the clerk. He sighed and put on his robe and wig, and he stepped into his black buckled shoes and followed the clerk up the stairs.

Down below Mildred could hear them, and she sent Marie-Tatin to tell Father William and David Chandler in the dining room. They came hurrying, and then the four climbed the stairs and stood near the jury room door. The clerk opened his mouth to object, but with Father William there in his full blacks, he changed his mind.

"What is it with you people?" they heard the judge say. He made no effort to keep his voice down. "What is the problem here? Were you not listening to my instructions?

What are your available choices, your considerations? Speak up, someone."

The foreman's voice said, "The charge is first-degree murder."

"Precisely. So? You must ask yourself, is she guilty of first-degree, yes or no? If you find that she is not, you move on. Madam Foreman, read me the legal definition of first-degree murder."

And they heard Mrs. Fitch clear her throat and stumble through a complicated legal paragraph.

"Stop right there," said the judge. "Repeat that phrase."

"Which one?"

"Madam!" shouted the judge. "Are we all awake here? The one you just read. 'Must contain an element, however small, of malice aforethought.' Think about it. *Taste* that notion. Hold it up to this case and do your job. If you do not find her guilty of first-degree, what about the included lesser charges? You've had nearly four hours already to deliberate, and so I'm going to carry this chair into the corner over there, and I'll sit and wait for twenty more minutes by my watch. You get to work and reach your verdict."

At 9:45 that night, the lights were turned on again in the co-operative market hall, and people when they saw that came from all over and stomped the snow off their boots and filed into the hall to stand behind the rope. The court scribe with his papers and pen came and sat at his desk, and then the assistant Crown attorney entered through the side door, followed by the matron and Hélène and Mr. Quormby. They all took their places and then the clerk told them to *rise, all rise*, and the Honourable Sir James F. Whitmore strode in, in his long black robe and big wig of office. Under his arm he carried his case notes.

He sat down in the chair behind his desk and said, "Clerk, proceed." And the clerk in his black suit and small wig stood very upright and declared this court to be in session. He said, "The accused will remain standing, but Crown and counsel may sit."

When all was quiet again, the judge said, "So bring in the jury," and the clerk stepped to the side-room door and opened it.

There were noises from the vegetable crates, and then the twelve men and women filed in, Mrs. Fitch the post-mistress first, and then the others, solemnly, with their hands behind their backs. They crossed the floor in front of the judge's desk to their chairs and sat down. They stopped moving, and for a few heartbeats there was not one sound inside or out on this snowy night.

Then the judge said, "Madam Foreman, has the jury reached a verdict?"

Mrs. Fitch was holding a piece of paper, and she put her hands on the armrests of her chair and stood up. She was very pale. They could all see her swallowing, and then she said, "Yes we have, Your Honour."

"And how do you find the accused in the charge of first-degree murder?"

And Mrs. Fitch said, "We find her not guilty, Your Honour. But—"

There came a collective sound from the audience, a loud sigh or exhalation, and the judge called, "Quiet! All quiet or I'll have the hall cleared." He turned to the jury and said, "Please continue, Madam Foreman."

Mrs. Fitch looked at the piece of paper in her hand, and then she raised her head. "But we do find her guilty of manslaughter, Your Honour. Manslaughter with reduced criminal culpability under the circumstances."

The judge allowed a moment's silence to give the verdict its due space. Then he leaned forward with his hands and elbows on the desk.

"So noted," he said. "Manslaughter. Thank you, Madam Foreman. Does the jury have a recommendation for a sentence?"

"We do, Your Honour. That same section in the code states that there is no set minimum sentence for manslaughter, and so we propose to give credit for the time in pre-trial confinement already served by the accused. But we also recommend an additional penalty of unpaid community work, which is listed in the code as an option, Your Honour. We recommend five hundred hours."

There was another silence, and then the judge said, "Very well. Five hundred hours' community work. This court agrees with the jury's recommendation. The community work is to be determined and monitored by local municipal authorities. Scribe, make note of it."

The judge paused. He looked around and said, "The court thanks the jury and the prosecution and the defence. This case is now closed. Madam, you are free to go. You will be contacted by your mayor's office."

He was looking fully at her then. A strong face, strong eyes. He inclined his head to her, and then hammered the gavel down on the wooden plate.

"Clerk," he said. "Have the motorcar brought around to the entrance."

Twenty-Nine

THE FIRST THING she did with her freedom the next morning was to put on her boots and coat and hat and walk to the post office to call Claire. In the street people smiled and said *Mornin', ma'am* and *Bonjour, Madame.*

It was just one week until Christmas.

On Sunday they performed the "Faith" cantata, and the church was filled again, and another hundred people stood outside in the snow. They were coming from all over now, straight across the peninsula from as far as Cape Sable and Port Mouton, a good three hours away in this weather, and Father William announced from the pulpit that for the next while there would be three services on Sundays: the first one at eight, High Mass at eleven, and vespers at seven. All with music and choir, he promised, although perhaps not always the full choir.

Claire was due to arrive on Wednesday, and this time Hélène drove to meet the ferry from Portland herself. She stopped at the foundry and asked David Chandler if he would like to come along and he said yes, he certainly would. He put down the piece he was working on and turned off the machines and went into the other room. He came back looking scrubbed and bright-eyed, his hair combed with water like a little boy.

They drove along the shore road with the evening sun veiled behind red clouds, and with slabs of ice on the water and seals and seagulls riding them.

"Are people leaving you alone about it, Mrs. Giroux?" he said. "I don't mean the newspaper people. I know they're still all over town, but everybody else."

"Yes, they are, Mr. Chandler. For the most part."

"And are you able to rest enough after the ordeal?"

"Yes, I am," she said. She told him she'd had an interesting telephone call at the church office. "Two, actually," she said. "From piano companies. Offers for management positions and quality control, one in Boston and one in Stratford, Ontario. I could be making pianos again, Mr. Chandler."

"Oh," he said.

After a while he said, "But would you want to be leaving here now?"

No, she wouldn't, she said. And she couldn't anyway, not with the ordered community work and the chance of organizing a music festival. There was a lot to think about, and it was much too soon to make any kind of decision.

"Of course," he said. "Can I ask a question, Mrs. Giroux? About the dinosaur skull."

"Of course, Mr. Chandler. Ask."

"What happened to it?"

"The government confiscated it. Apparently they had just passed a law forbidding private ownership of fossil finds. Nathan might not have known, but I think the geologist did, and that's why we never saw him in person. I imagine someday that skull will end up in a British museum. Maybe it has already. I do know that they sent over a mythologist and a team from London, and they took away one of the rock pyramids and shipped it to England and erected it in a museum."

"Imagine," he said. "And one last thing, Mrs. Giroux. The dog, what happened to it?"

"Jack. He ended up at that outfitter's where we rented him. All the other dogs did too, they just found their way home. I inquired about that once, but I never went back."

They were standing among other people on the Yarmouth pier by then, waiting for the ferry.

She said, "When I was young I always wanted a dog, but I could never have one. Jack was the best dog anyone could wish for. He was strong and fierce and loyal. And he could smile, Mr. Chandler. I saw that with my own eyes."

It was night and a few overhead lights on wires were on. If they shielded their eyes they could see the ferry, not far out now: bright windows, the small red and green lights at port and starboard. The running lights at the mast. The ferry came their way through the night, pushing before it a wave of foaming water. It sounded its horn.

Much of that week leading up to Christmas, the weather was clear and cold. Truckloads of Christmas trees had been delivered to the square, and people came with their children and bought trees and took them home on toboggans. Then it began to snow again. Blue jays screeched and dipped between bird feeders, and at noon on Thursday winter lightning could be seen in the middle of the day and then thunder rolled over the town. Market stalls sold roasted chestnuts and tea and home-baked cookies and fudge and mulled wine. Sergeant Elliott came to inspect liquor licences, and when they did not have one he said they would have to stop selling mulled wine, but that they could wait until the writ was served, which might take a week or more with him being so busy.

They rehearsed the Christmas concert for hours. They had decided to drop the part of the Bach oratorio, and they would instead focus on carols. She'd considered bringing in some strings, but there was not enough time to rehearse. Father William agreed it was better to keep things simple for now.

"But in the new year," he said and smiled. "The French Shore Music Festival. I do look forward to that. I mentioned our idea to the mayor, and he said he would talk to the councillors. He was very interested."

Claire had eight days before she needed to fly back. She'd had a call letting her know that the position was hers; now she was thinking of building on it and then perhaps going back to university for a full medical degree. She spent her nights bunking on the sofa in the living room, and every night on her way to the bathroom Hélène would glance through the doorway towards the sofa in the window light and feel a sweet pain in her heart and move on.

Claire borrowed skates and with other young people went to the rink behind the school. She also took on the job of dealing with the reporters; too many of them were still in town, snooping around and clicking pictures of Hélène whenever they glimpsed her. It took a few days, but Claire confronted them one by one and asked them kindly to leave her mother alone now. And one after another, they did.

For Mass on Christmas Eve, she'd wear the long dark-grey skirt and the matching jacket over a white blouse, silk stockings and her mother's pearls. She'd laid the clothes out on the bed, and she was in the kitchen making tea when Father William came up to see her.

"Have a cup of tea," she said. "I've got some brewing."

He followed her into the kitchen and they pulled out chairs. He seemed different somehow. Upset about something.

"Is everything all right?" she said.

"Ah. No, it is not." He took a deep breath and let it out. "How do I say this? Mrs. Giroux, ever since you told me about your father's death and the missionaries, I have been very understanding with you. Very tolerant. But now I have a problem that I cannot ignore."

"Tell me."

"The problem is that, while it was at first all right for you to be uncommitted, now your admission in public of a criminal act – no, let me finish – your admission of an act the church calls a mortal sin, calls for certain steps to be taken. I think you know what I mean."

"At the time, you told me that I was not the only uncommitted one in your congregation. And you did not mind. Or 'you did and you didn't,' if I remember correctly."

"Yes, yes. But, the difference, Mrs. Giroux – surely you can see that. The difference is that the other uncommitted people haven't just admitted that they killed another human being. And they are not sitting at our piano, right in front for all the congregation to see – in a place of privilege – making our sacred music at Mass."

That silenced her for a moment.

"I hadn't thought of it that way," she said then.

"Hadn't you."

"No. What do you want me to do?"

"It's not what *I* want you to do. It's what the church requires of you. You must be seen at confession. You must be seen to be contrite. And you must be seen doing penance. Three steps."

"Even if I don't believe in them?"

"Yes. Even then. Let's put that aside for now. In any case, there is always hope. Until the last breath, we are told."

"And what was that final day of the trial if not one long confession? And contrition and genuine sorrow."

"That was altogether different, and you know it."

"As far as I'm concerned, it comes to exactly the same thing in the end. *Exactly.* But never mind."

"Yes. Never mind." He stood up. "Mrs. Giroux, the issue has been weighing on me ever since the verdict. It pains me to say it, but I have made my decision, and here it is: I can give you the rest of today and tomorrow to think about it, but if you have not done publicly by then what is required of you now, I cannot allow you to provide our music any more. In that case, tonight would be your last time at our piano."

And so at five o'clock she stood in line with all the others at the confessional, and they nodded at her and looked at one another with raised eyebrows.

When she was on the kneeling bench with the curtain closed and her window not yet open, she could hear him whispering towards the other side. Then that window slid shut and hers opened, and he glanced at her and leaned close to the screen to listen. Afterward he made the sign of the cross between them. He murmured in Latin, and the sweet, earnest simplicity of it all took her back to her childhood in Montmagny, to her first communion, when her father had been home, and it nearly broke her heart all over again.

For penance he gave her two Lord's Prayers and three Hail Marys, and she walked to a pew and sat with her eyes closed, hunched over the bible rail in the cold church saying them.

In the hotel kitchen, the women were preparing three strings of carp for dinner for the strict Catholics over the holidays. For all the others they'd be roasting several turkeys and geese. Side dishes would be Brussels sprouts done in garlic and butter, squash and turnip and sweet potatoes and sugar peas and mashed field potatoes, all from the fall harvest in the Annapolis Valley. Dessert would be a compote of pears and wild blueberries stewed with maple syrup and a splash of raisin rum. All local food, most of it donated like every year. Mildred had hired four more helpers, women who'd just the other day been laid off again at the Quaker, and she'd put Marie-Tatin in charge of them.

"Now, mind," Mildred overheard Marie-Tatin say to the new ones. "Mrs. Yamoussouke, she wants things done quite particular in her kitchen. You'll be startin' with the vegetables and I'll be tellin' you how, so please listen."

During midnight Mass she sat at the piano waiting for Father William to give her the sign. From where she sat she could see Claire and David Chandler, side by side in a pew. She had already asked him, and he'd said he would be very pleased to sit between them for the meal at the hotel on Christmas Day.

"And Mrs. Giroux," he'd said with a smile. "Do you think it might be possible for you and me to use first names? From this Christmas on, perhaps. Would you agree? I would like that very much."

"Oh, for heaven's sake, David," she'd said. "Of course. I would like it too."

Claire looked so beautiful in that light. She looked a lot like Pierre, something about her jawline and the way she held her head. But also like Mother somehow, around the eyes.

She thought of her mother and of her mother's face, and how much it had calmed her to see Father Dubert in her last hours. All anxiety gone in an instant. He'd parted the curtains and appeared in his full vestments like a king walking into a desert tent with all the power to bring peace, and she'd stood up from the chair and moved back while he went down on one knee and knelt at Mother's bed.

"*In nomine Patris, et Filii, et Spiritus Sancti . . .*," he'd said.

So strange. Quite wonderful.

She sat with her hands in her lap, kneading them a bit to keep them warm, and just before the second set of carols, Morris turned off half the lights from the row of switches by the side altar, and he came forward and with a pinewood taper lit the eight candles along the communion rail.

It was so absolutely still in the church that they could hear the crackling of the small flame.

Everyone was watching as the wicks caught the light one by one, and when Morris had blown out the taper and moved back into the shadows, Father William turned to her and gave the tiniest of nods.

Acknowledgements

I wish to thank Jacques Franklin, old-world *accordeur*, who years ago in Africa introduced me to the secret world of pianos, and who knew all about the art in the craft. Thank you also to Lara Hinchberger, my editor, who brought a great deal to this story; to Ellen Seligman my publisher; and to Ellen Levine, my agent. Thank you to our friends Lynne and Tony Prower for sharing some of their musical knowledge, and to Phyl and Don Ketcheson for the many fine musical moments at their house, and for letting me tinker with their Bechstein. And a very big thank-you to you, Heather, always my first reader.

Please go to
www.penguinrandomhouse.ca
to find a book club kit for
The Piano Maker, including:

- A story by the author about events
  and encounters that inspired him to write
  this novel
- A reading group guide with suggested
  questions
- Book-themed ideas for topics at your book
  club meeting

KURT PALKA is the author of seven novels. His previous work includes *Clara*, which was published in hardcover as *Patient Number 7* and was a finalist for the Hammett Prize, and most recently *The Hour of the Fox*. He lives near Toronto.